Sharon J. Clark grew up
Staffordshire, and now l
two sons, a cat named J;
hunter, and the grumpie
Earth.

She has been a writer from the moment she first grasped a
coloured crayon. This collection of short stories spans
more than 20 years, and is a mix of previously published
work and brand new fiction. She has also written a novel
(not yet published) and she is working on a second.
Meanwhile, she helps to pay the bills (two sons at
university!) by working as an editor at a well-known
educational establishment.

In her spare time, Sharon supports the work of Mercy in
Action (www.mercyinaction.org.uk) and travels as much as
time and money allow.

# The Chocolate Box

Sharon J. Clark

iConnect Books

# Acknowledgements

I owe a huge debt of gratitude to Judy M. without whom this book simply would not be; to Karen Miller, who will forever be an inspiration; to Cindee Phillips for her friendship, support and words of wisdom; and to Judy B., who has offered sound advice, generous hospitality and an unswerving loyalty and friendship beyond what I deserve.

For my mother

I miss you

# Contents

## Musical Memories

Something was wrong. Madeleine could tell from the sounds in the hallway. There were two soft thuds – Edward's saxophone case hitting the floor followed by the briefcase that held his music. Then there was a weary exhalation. Her fingers rubbed away a barely visible smudge on the glass-topped coffee table in front of her as she listened. The clock on the mantelpiece ticked loudly, and then she heard him move to the coat closet – a soft rustle as he hung up his jacket, the twin sounds of the cases being set in their places.

She moved from the lounge to the kitchen, going through the dining room so as not to disturb him as he took off his shoes. Surrounded by the cosy warmth of primrose yellow walls, she switched the kettle on, and then busied herself with cups and teabags. "You're back early," she called to him, keeping her voice light. The closet door closed with a harsh click.

"Aye. The young 'uns went for a drink, but I thought it best to get back before the roads got icy."

That was odd. Madeleine frowned as she reached for the biscuit tin. "Wasn't the forecast for mild weather tonight?"

He didn't answer. Just an excuse, then. A chill that had nothing to do with the temperature settled around her as she put two of his favourite biscuits on his saucer, and carried his tea through to him. Something was definitely wrong. Had been for the past few Thursday evenings now.

"So how was the practice?" she asked as she put his cup and saucer on the table.

He nodded his thanks, and then stabbed a shortbread finger into his tea. "We did more of that modern rubbish Joe Tanner likes so much."

Madeleine winced at the name. Joe Tanner was the new bandleader. He taught music at the local high school

9

and had been the obvious successor when Fred Parker's rheumatism had forced him to retire. "You two not getting on?"

"What?" Edward's gaze jerked from the television. "No, it's not like that. It's just the music. Nothing but a load of notes flung together at random if you ask me."

She relaxed. If that was all that was bothering him, it was easily fixed. "Have you talked to him?"

"Talked about what?"

"The repertoire." Sometimes Edward was purposefully dense. Obviously he hadn't spoken to Tanner. He most likely didn't want to discuss it with her either. Well, the latter was too bad. Problem solving was what she did in the family. Always had. Always would. "Edward?" she prompted when he didn't reply.

Another sigh escaped him. "What's the point? He's the bandleader. What he says goes. And besides, everyone else thinks he's the best thing to ever happen to the band. They're all excited about doing festivals and stuff." He turned back to the news. "He writes a lot of that stuff himself, you know."

"Well, that's all well and good," she said. "But surely there's room for some of the traditional tunes too?"

Edward swallowed the last mouthful of his tea. His eyes never moved from the television screen as he spoke. "I'm thinking of giving it up."

"Stop playing with the band?" The notion was shocking. He'd been part of the City Jazz Band their whole married life. He was virtually a founding member.

He glanced at her and for a moment she saw the distress in his eyes. "Can't do a thing forever, Maddy. Just ask Fred Parker."

"But you love playing."

He didn't answer. Simply shrugged his shoulders as though it was nothing important. Then he reached for the TV remote and notched the sound higher. Conversation over.

Annoyed, she went into the kitchen and did what she always did when she was upset – started to clean. Damn Joe Tanner and his modern ideas. How could he do this? Edward wasn't some piece of dirt to be wiped away, erased as though he never existed. The band had always been an important part of his life. When he retired from work the Thursday night rehearsal had become one of the high spots of his week. Just who did Tanner think he was?

By the time she'd mopped an already spotless floor her mind was made up. If Edward wouldn't talk to Tanner, she would.

The bus dropped her at the school gate fifteen minutes early. The last time she'd visited the place, her youngest son had been in his teens and excited about going off to university. It was odd to think that he was attending parent evenings of his own now. The building hadn't changed much. The interior walls were still the colour of cold porridge, the smell of damp clothes pervaded the corridors, and it was as maze-like as ever. It was a wonder anyone ever found the right classrooms.

Eventually, though, she arrived outside the music room, and used the few remaining minutes of the school day to assess her enemy though the glass panelling in the door. Joe Tanner was pacing at the front of the class, energetically delivering a lecture that she couldn't quite hear. He was in his mid-thirties, dressed in the same jeans and t-shirt uniform as his students, and constantly pushing a strand of long dark hair out of his eyes. Oh, for a pair of scissors.

Her gaze moved to his students. Well, that was a surprise. Every single one of them was staring at him in rapt attention. It was entirely possible, of course, that one or two of the girls were simply appreciating 'the eye candy'. That was what they called nice-looking young men, wasn't it? However, getting the whole class under his spell

11

probably spoke more about his teaching ability than his looks.

The ring of a bell heralded a stampede. Madeleine flattened herself against the corridor wall suddenly afraid of being swept away in a tide of teenagers. When finally it was safe she knocked politely on the classroom door. Tanner glanced up, surprise morphing into a welcoming smile. "Hello."

"Mr Tanner." She held out her hand as she approached. "I'm Madeleine Baker."

"A pleasure to meet you." He shook her hand, frowning slightly as though trying to place her name. "Are you here about one of my students?"

"No. I wanted to talk to you about my husband. Edward Baker. He plays in the City Jazz Band."

"Edward? Ah! You're Ted's wife. How can I help you?"

"It's about the band, Mr Tanner. I'll be blunt because I've found that's always the best approach. I'm concerned that Edward isn't enjoying it any more, and I wondered if you'd noticed anything."

Tanner curled his bottom lip over his top one as he thought. Then he shook his head. "I'm sorry, Mrs Baker, but I can't say I have."

"He hasn't said anything to you about giving up?"

"Good grief, no." Tanner looked shocked. "He's told you he wants to do that?"

"He mentioned it last night." At least Tanner didn't welcome the news. That was good. It gave her a bargaining chip of sorts.

Tanner ran a hand through his hair again. "Do you know why?"

Oh yes, she knew exactly what the reason was. If he was half the leader that Fred Parker had been, he'd have known too. She met his gaze. "Since taking over as band leader you've made quite a lot of changes to the repertoire. Is that right?"

12

"Yes, but…"

She cut him off. "Mr Tanner, my husband has been a member of the City Jazz Band for over twenty years. In all that time, traditional jazz has been the mainstay of the band's repertoire. It's why people pay good money to listen to them. And it's what the band likes to play."

He perched himself on the edge of his desk. "It's what Ted likes to play, you mean."

"Not just Edward…"

He raised a hand, his forefinger wagging. Oh yes, he was a teacher alright. "Mrs Baker, there's something you need to know about the band. When Fred Parker retired, most of the older members went too. The only way to keep it going was to recruit new members, and that's what I've done." He gestured towards the empty classroom. "Several of the students who were here earlier are now a part of it and, as you can imagine, they tend to lean towards more modern trends."

"And that's all that matters?" She winced at the bitterness in her tone, but she couldn't deny the feeling. Out with the old, in with the new. It was an all-too familiar pattern.

He shook his head. "Of course not, but they are the future. Without them, where do you think the City Jazz Band will be in six months, a year?" His face was earnest. The words delivered not to hurt, but with a passion for what he was doing. "I don't want to see twenty years of tradition end any more than you do, Mrs Baker. I want this band to continue, building on all that Fred Parker and your husband have put into it."

She suddenly felt foolish and petty. Too caught up in her own tiny world to have considered that there might be a much bigger issue than Edward's enjoyment. She'd tried to fight a battle that didn't exist. Had assumed Edward had kept quiet because Tanner was a thoughtless bully, when the opposite was in fact true. "I didn't realise. I'm sorry, I shouldn't have come." She held out her hand, an act of capitulation as well as farewell. "I wish you all the best, Mr Tanner."

"Does Ted really want to leave?" he asked. He was holding her hand now, keeping her from leaving. The skin of his palm was warm against hers. "Couldn't you talk to him?"

"To what end?"

"Persuade him to stay. To give the new repertoire a go. It would be good for the kids to have him around. They tend to glaze over when I talk about the history of jazz, but Ted… well, he's lived it, and somehow he's able to make it come alive." He gave a soft laugh. "And apart from all that, I'd really appreciate knowing I could rely on at least one person in the band to turn up on time."

She found herself nodding, and almost laughed at the easy way he'd turned her from enemy to ally. Charisma. That was what she'd seen at work earlier. And what would make the City Jazz Band go on to new heights provided he had the right support.

"I'll see what I can do," she said.

"Why don't you give some of that new music a go?" she asked as casually as she could. It was Saturday afternoon, and force of habit had made Edward settle down to an hour of practice. He gave her an odd look and she kicked herself for the less than subtle approach.

"Call that music?" he replied.

"You might like it once you're familiar with it." The argument seemed reasonable. Edward apparently didn't agree, though. He made a rude noise and continued with the piece he was playing, not even looking at the sheet music because he knew the notes so well. Madeleine began to polish the furniture. The moment he hit the final note, she tried again. "Don't you get bored playing the same old thing? I know I'd like to hear something fresh." To her disappointment, though, he started on yet another well-known tune. So much for hoping he might try something

14

different for her. Time for more direct action. Setting aside her duster, she began to rummage through his briefcase.

He stopped in mid-song. "What are you doing?"

"Looking for something I don't know."

"Why?"

"Don't you want a challenge occasionally?"

"Maddy, what's going on?"

"Nothing. I just thought it would be nice to hear you play something different. Perhaps some of the modern stuff?" Her fingers folded around a photocopied sheet of handwritten music. "What about this?"

Edward made a rude noise. However, he took the music from her. "Very well. But only for you." She smiled to herself as she went back to polishing. Moments later, though, the vibrant notes of the saxophone stopped. Edward cursed to himself, and started again. Another halt. Another restart. And then abruptly he snatched the music off the stand, screwed it up into a ball and hurled it towards the wastepaper bin. It bounced off the lip and rolled onto the middle of the rug in front of the fire. "Stupid piece of rubbish." He glared at it.

Not good. Not good at all. Madeleine retrieved the music, uncrumpled it and began to smooth it out. "It just needs a little more practice, is all."

The glare turned to her. "Why this sudden interest in what I play?"

Heat burned her cheeks. Edward wasn't a fool. And he knew her better than anyone. "I told you…"

"Maddy." It was more a growl than speech.

She'd overstepped the mark, and she knew it. Besides, she never was any good at keeping things from him. "I went to see Joe Tanner."

"What?"

Oh dear. This was not turning out at all well. A row was the last thing she wanted. "Don't be mad with me, Edward. I was just trying to help. The past few weeks, you've been so miserable after band practice. I thought perhaps I could persuade him to go back to doing the tunes you love."

The heat of his gaze moved to the music in her hand. It was a wonder the paper didn't catch light. "Let me guess. Instead of you persuading him, he convinced you to try and talk me round to playing that rubbish." She couldn't deny it. Knew that her face told him the answer. He snorted. "Did he tell you about all the teenagers he's recruited? They're all under his spell as well."

"He's doing his best to keep the band alive, Edward."

"Is that right." The bitterness was sweetened by a weary resignation.

"And I was just trying to help. I hate seeing you so miserable." She held the smoothed music out to him. "Please, won't you at least try?"

"No." His chin raised stubbornly, and she knew she'd lost. Once Edward got that look on his face, there was no persuading him.

Irritation pricked at her. Stubborn fool. "At least tell me why not. Are you upset that he's the band leader and you're not?"

"Don't be ridiculous. You know I've never had any ambition in that area."

"Then what? Do you really hate this music so much that you'd rather not play anything?"

He stared at her for a long moment, as though trying to decide if it was worth the effort of explaining. Finally he made a dismissive flick of his hand at the page she was holding. "That modern stuff, it makes me feel... old."

The word hung between them, darkly malevolent. She stared at his saxophone and saw the rich golden sheen of metal that had been lovingly polished over the years. And she heard the notes he'd played earlier, lifting effortlessly into the air. His fingers had danced up and down the keys as though of their own accord. And suddenly she understood. The old, familiar tunes were a part of him. Years of practice and repetition meant he could probably

16

play them in his sleep. Joe Tanner's compositions required effort and shone a spotlight on a body that was no longer as agile as perhaps it once had been.

Slowly she crumpled the music up again. This time it found the wastepaper basket. "I shouldn't have interfered."

He didn't reply, but she knew from the look on his face that he agreed with her. First she'd failed with Tanner. Now with Edward. So much for her problem solving abilities.

The silence was killing her. For two whole weeks not a single note of jazz had been played in the house. Edward's saxophone remained in its case in the closet. Thursday came and went. Came and went again. Meanwhile the house gleamed as she cleaned and polished with the kind of vigour that was really only warranted for a forthcoming visit from the queen. There had to be a way for Edward to continue playing and enjoying it. There just had to be. Yet, no matter how often she cleaned the kitchen floor, a solution simply refused to come to her. Then, one afternoon as she was brushing nonexistent cobwebs off the photo frames in the lounge, she suddenly realised the answer was staring her in the face. It was a risky idea. And if Edward wanted to be stubborn then there really wouldn't be anything else she could do. But it was the only avenue left.

It took a bit of planning, but Fred Parker was only too happy to pretend he needed Edward's help with some DIY that would keep him busy until dinner time. On Edward's return, she hurried him into the dining room where a homemade steak pie was waiting for him. He always praised her pastry, and tonight was no exception. When they'd finished eating he helped her clear away the dishes and then she waited nervously in the kitchen as he headed for the lounge. She heard the door open. The silence that followed seemed to last forever. Hadn't he noticed? Or was he choosing not to? She made a cup of tea, added two of his favourite biscuits to the saucer and carried it through to him.

He was standing by the fire, which she'd lit earlier. He turned to her, a confused expression on his face. "Why is my saxophone out?"

She put the tea cup on the table and then sat on the sofa. "I was hoping you'd play for me. I've put our favourite tune on the music stand."

He stared at the waiting instrument for a long moment, and then crossed the room and read the song title aloud. "Someone to watch over me." The words bought a smile to his face; a smile that spoke of a lifetime of marriage. Of good times and bad times.

She returned the look with an encouraging one of her own. "Please, Edward. The house has been so quiet of late. Won't you play for me?"

Across the room, Edward picked up his saxophone, fingers caressing the cold, smooth metal. Madeleine looked away and saw instead the photograph behind him. The one that had given her hope that there was still a solution. It had been taken in the mid 1960s, back in the early days of the band when Edward and Fred Parker still daydreamed of one day playing at Ronnie Scott's club. A time before paying the mortgage and putting food on the table had ensured that their love of jazz would only ever be a hobby rather than a career. Edward had been handsome in his youth, at least in her eyes. He still was. And he still played the familiar old songs like a dream.

Soft, mellow notes suddenly filled the lounge as Edward bought the saxophone to life. The notes turned into a song. And the song swelled into something far richer as he endowed each note with passion and love. Both for the music. And for her.

When the final bar had been played, Edward set the saxophone down and sighed. A long, satisfied sigh. "I

**18**

phoned Joe Tanner earlier in the week. I've already told him I'm not going back to the band," he said.

She crossed the room and wrapped her arms around him. "Are you sure that's the right decision?"

"Positive." He gave another sigh, as though casting off a heavy weight. Then he smiled. "You never guess what he asked me to do, though?"

"What?"

"Wants me to go into the school and talk to his students about jazz history. Reckons I'd be good at it."

Madeleine smiled. "I think you'd be very good at it. What did you tell him?"

"Said I'd think about it. I reckon I'll probably do it, though. At least, give it a go, see what it's like. A challenge, right?"

"I'm very proud of you," she said. "But will you promise me one thing?"

"If I can."

"Will you still play for me? Every Thursday? Just the two of us."

He pressed his lips to the top of her head as he drew her closer. "You were always the only person in the audience I was really playing for."

His words warmed her heart as she rested her head on his shoulder. He began to hum 'Someone to watch over me'. Madeleine softly started to sing.

And together they waltzed slowly around the lounge.

## The Ups and Downs of Life

What was she thinking? She was far too old to be even contemplating this. It was madness. Complete madness.

"Come on, Mum!"

That was Todd. Seventeen years old. And totally fearless.

He whizzed past her, his skis hissing like king cobras. Irritation flared as she watched him zigzag effortlessly down the slope. It was all so unfair. "I'm only doing this for you, you know. I wasn't the one that wanted to come skiing," she shouted. The words went unheard. The sacrifice unappreciated. "And don't think I've forgotten how rude you were at breakfast either." Might as well air all the complaints of the day while she was at it.

She glowered at the glistening white expanse before her. Surely it was way too steep to be a beginner's run. Mountain climbing equipment seemed more appropriate than skis.

*Fear is the mind killer.* It was a favourite quote from a science fiction novel she'd read as a teenager. She repeated it to herself. Right, she could do this. She'd had lessons. Three of them – at the indoor slope in her home town. Despite spending more time sitting in the snow than gliding gracefully over it, her instructor had promised her that she knew enough to enjoy this holiday. Yeah, right. He wasn't the mother of two cocky teenage boys and a husband who had gone from beginner to Olympic standard in the same time she'd gone from totally incompetent to Ski Slope Scud Missile: fast and straight with a big crash at the end.

Tentatively she shuffled forward, and then made a wedge shape with her skis the way she'd been shown. And... her heartbeat accelerated at the same rate as her speed. Oh no. Too fast. Much too fast! And she was

21

heading straight for the trees. Got to slow down. Got to stop!

Her instructor's voice was yelling inside her head as a sudden desperate desire to live took over from the panic.

Phew!

She came to a shuddery halt. Eyes squeezed tightly closed, she took a deep breath and tried to calm the trembling in her knees. Seconds later there was the distinctive whoosh of someone coming to a halt right behind her.

"Come on, Mum! Haven't you made it to the bottom yet?"

She opened her eyes, and forced her lips into a smile that was no doubt more of a grimace. "I'm just enjoying the scenery."

Todd laughed. "You're facing the trees."

"I happen to like trees." Cautiously she turned, poles firmly stuck in the snow to prevent any unwanted downward motion.

Todd grinned happily. "Race you down!" He was off again, hips sashaying with the kind of grace that'd had teenage girls of her generation swooning over Patrick Swayze in Dirty Dancing.

The maternal side of her character whispered that she should be glad he was enjoying himself. Unfortunately her selfish side had hijacked a megaphone and was engaged in a full volume diatribe about the ignorance of teenage boys. Couldn't he see that she was hating every minute of this? If she ever managed to make it down this slope…

'For goodness sake, stop whinging woman!' That was her rational side, arriving just in time to prevent thoughts of infanticide. Or rather teenicide.

Right. Get a grip. She was a grown woman. She held down a demanding job. She'd run the London Marathon for charity. And been through childbirth. Twice, for goodness sake. No stupid ski slope on some stupid Swiss mountain was going to beat her.

Deep breath. Keep the upper body still. Push forward and turn. And… No! The toes of her skis crossed. There wasn't even time for a decent panic. The world simply did a sickening loop-the-loop, and then she was lying face down on the snow in a sprawl that gave a whole new meaning to inelegant.

A pair of skis appeared mere inches from her nose. Perhaps a gorgeous Swiss ski instructor to her rescue? No. She groaned as she recognised the face beneath the yellow-tinted goggles. What had she done to deserve this? It was Simon, her younger son. Almost fifteen, he had yet to discover that compassion was more than just a word in the dictionary.

"Fallen over?" he asked.

She sucked in enough breath to force out a coherent sentence. "Just stopped for a rest."

His grin was cheekier than his brother's, and just as unwelcome. "See you at the bottom. Try not to bring all the snow down with you."

"Who appointed you snow monitor?" she growled.

He angled his skis downhill and was gone. Wretched boys. How come they found it so easy? Must be their father's genes. Clearly weren't hers.

Rolling over, she lay on her back and stared up at the sky. It was a vibrant Mediterranean blue; a beautiful cloudless azure that whispered of golden beaches, shady palm trees and deliciously fruity Chianti. Now that would be a holiday.

That was it. She was done with skiing. Once down the beginner's slope. Five falls. Twenty minutes of white-knuckled terror.

"Mum. Mum! Where are you going?"

She pretended not to hear Todd calling to her. Carrying her skis balanced on her right shoulder, she waddled towards the distant line of coffee shops. The rigid soles of her ski boots didn't lend themselves to a graceful exit. Nor a swift one.

"Mum!" Todd caught up with her, sliding effortlessly across the snow. "Where are you going?"

"For coffee." She ducked her head down and slogged on.

"Already?"

"Yes, already." The skis were heavy on her shoulder. Sweat was trickling down her back, and her boots were cutting into her ankles. Abruptly she pulled to a halt. "Look, I only agreed to this holiday because you and your brother whined on and on about wanting to ski. I could quite happily have lived my entire life without ever doing… this!" Her ski poles rattled as she made a sweeping gesture that encompassed the slopes, the lifts and the confident tots racing past her like seasoned professionals. "Just go and enjoy yourself. I'll be fine."

A forlorn look crossed his face, and suddenly she felt bad for snapping at him. Now who was acting like a thoughtless teenager? "Sorry," she said. "This just isn't my thing, okay? Go have fun. That's what matters."

He stared at her for a moment, more thoughtful than she ever recalled. Then he shifted his weight from one ski to the other, and adopted a nonchalant expression. "I could show you the best way down, if you wanted."

The offer startled her, and not just because it would involve going back up the slope. Mr Think-Only-About-Himself was offering to help? Had someone kidnapped her real son and replaced him with an impostor? She blinked at him, then matched his nonchalance with casualness. "There's a best way?"

He nodded. "If you go straight down the middle it's way too fast. But if you use the banks at the sides, it's easier."

She turned and stared at the Slope of Doom. Then she looked at her son's face. Oh heck, she was probably going to regret it, but she never had been able to refuse those puppy dog eyes. "Okay." She dropped her skis onto the snow and stamped her boots back into the grips. "Just for you."

It really was very pretty at the top of the piste. But the slope looked as evil as ever. Todd waited beside her as she fiddled with her gloves and her poles and her goggles and anything else she could think of to put off the dreaded moment when she had to move.

"Ready?" he asked patiently.

Not really, but she didn't say so. Instead she gave a grim-faced nod.

"Right," he said. "See that slight rise across the slope there?"

She peered into the dazzling sunlight and noticed for the first time that the side of the piste was indeed banked. "Yes, what about it?"

"If you ski towards it, the incline will slow you down as you turn. Then come back across the slope and do the same on the other side. When we get to that tree, we'll stop." He gestured a short distance down the slope. "Okay?"

To her surprise, he was making a lot of sense. "Okay."

"Right," he said. "Follow me. Nice wide wedge to keep your speed down." She watched him carefully. Saw how he turned on the slope of the bank. Okay. Form a wedge shape. Push forward and across the slope and... Yes. This was controlled skiing. She reached the bank, turned smoothly and traversed back. Another turn and a smooth stop at the tree. Todd grinned at her. "Cool! Ready for the next bit?"

She nodded, still nervous, but with the growing suspicion that she'd just been shown one of the secrets of skiing that had been obvious to everyone except her. Todd gestured down the slope with one of his poles, pointing out the places to turn in order to use the natural topography to provide extra control. A few moments later,

25

they set off, this time coming to rest just before a large, orange padded pole.

"Okay?" he asked.

"Yes." More than okay. She'd actually enjoyed that bit. Once again, he pointed out the route and led the way. Once again she followed, concentrating on everything she'd learnt in her lessons and refusing to let the panic get the better of her when the speed suddenly notched up. When she came to a halt this time, she felt a smile tugging at her lips.

But then, she looked at the final section. This bit really was steep and there were no helpful banks to break the turns on. "Chill," Todd said. "This is the fun part. Just go for it."

"I won't be able to stop," she protested, looking at the base of the slope where other skiers were expertly coming straight off the slope and joining the lift queue.

"Yes you will," he said. "Just keep in a wedge shape and turn either right or left at the bottom. The snow is deeper there. It'll stop you."

"Really?"

"Trust me."

Trust me. How many times had she said that to him? A mother to a child. Something caught in her chest. A fluttering emotion attached to the knowledge that her son was growing up, that their relationship had changed without her even noticing. She took a deep breath and felt the cold mountain air fill her lungs. And then she was moving, pushing out with her knees, keeping her skis in the all-important wedge. Faster and faster, her heart racing, nerves singing. A loud whoop tore from her throat. Exhilaration. Triumph. Excitement. Then she was at the bottom, concentrating on leaning her weight forward over her right toe in order to carve a turn.

"I did it!" She punched the air, grinning wildly.

"Sure did," Todd said.

She reached out, and pulled him to her in a hug. "Thank you!'

For once he didn't shrug her off. "Think you can do it on your own now?"

She looked up the Slope of Doom. It didn't seem that high anymore. Or that steep. "Reckon I can give it a try."

"Cool!"

And with that he was off, his attention caught by two pretty Swiss girls waiting in the lift queue.

Still smiling, she took the lift to the top. Then, slowly but surely, skied to bottom. Todd shot past her in the last five yards, closely followed by the girls.

"Hey, my mum can ski," he called.

Yes, she thought, as she came to a halt at the bottom. Mum has learnt to ski. And despite the teenage swagger, apparently you've learnt a few things too. Good things like patience and thoughtfulness.

She smiled to herself. Perhaps coming on this holiday wasn't so bad after all.

## The Walker

"A room for tonight? I'm sorry. We're full." Win's attention flicked to the board that announced her home was also Rose Garden Guesthouse. The 'Vacancies' sign swung beneath it, a silent reproach. Oh dear. "I should've taken the sign down this morning." Second time this week she'd forgotten to do that. Brain like a sieve.

The young woman standing before her gave a small shrug. "It's okay. I ought to have booked ahead. It will serve me right if I end up sleeping in a barn or something."

"A barn? Goodness me. No need for that." Win leaned forward, intending to point out the Dougals' guesthouse, a few yards further down the lane. They always had spare rooms. However, there was something about this girl that made her pause. Perhaps it was the blonde hair and slim build, so like her daughter's. Maybe it was her anxious glance at the gate – as though expecting a monster to leap from the rose bushes and gobble her up. Or perhaps it was simply the thought of inflicting the Dougals on yet another innocent tourist. Whatever the reason, she turned the gesture into one of a hand offered in welcome. "Maybe I can squeeze you in. I'm Win."

"Katie." The young woman shook her hand. A surprisingly firm grip. "Thanks. I'm too impulsive for my own good sometimes."

"Well, I'm afraid the only room I have is rather small." Win unhooked the 'Vacancies' sign, setting it on the battered writing desk in the hall as Katie followed her through the front door. "And the décor isn't exactly… well, perhaps you'd best see for yourself." She led the way up the stairs and then opened a door at the end of a narrow hallway, revealing a pocket-sized bedroom. Bright sunlight gushed through the window, making the poppy red and daffodil yellow on the walls even more garish than normal. She winced an apology. "It's my granddaughter's room. She visits in the school holidays and, well, she chose the wallpaper herself."

"It's absolutely perfect," Katie said.

Perfect for a five-year-old maybe. "There is another guesthouse in the village if you'd rather." Of course, if the girl was one minute late for breakfast, Myra Dougal would make her displeasure known for a week. However, the Dougals' passion for time-keeping didn't really make it right to crush a guest into a boxroom.

"No, really. This is fine."

More impulsiveness? Or perhaps she simply didn't care where she stayed. Win suspected the latter from the cursory glance Katie had given the room before dropping her rucksack on the floor by the bed. "Well, if you're sure."

"I am." The reply was quick, as though she was afraid Win might change her mind about letting the room.

"Just the one night, is it?"

Katie walked two short strides to the window and stood with her back to Win. "Yes. No. That is, I'm not really sure to be honest." She glanced over her shoulder. "Do you need to know in advance?"

"Well, I don't usually let this room. So no, you don't have to make up your mind right now."

Katie turned back to the window. "I used to walk these hills with my dad when I was a kid. Kind of felt the need to – I don't know – just come back." She faced Win again, and smiled rather wistfully. "It's so peaceful out there, isn't it?"

Oh dear. Was her father dead? She wouldn't be the first to make a pilgrimage in the memory of a loved one. And yet... no, that couldn't be right. There was a nervousness about her that didn't fit with someone in mourning. Win returned the smile. Now wasn't the time to be asking a dozen nosey questions, even if Katie did look like she needed a good hug. "Aye," she said. "Though it's been a while since I dragged myself out on the hills."

30

Katie raised her eyebrows. "If I lived here, I think I'd walk every day. In fact, that's what I'm going to do right now." She spun round, tugged open her rucksack and pulled out a pair of well-worn boots.

Win laughed. "Aye, you're an impulsive one, alright."

Katie's smile vanished. "Except when it really matters." With that she turned her back on Win, and busied herself with her boot laces.

The abrupt end to the conversation didn't bother Win. All sorts came through her door. Some left as friends. Some never got more intimate than a polite good morning greeting. She treated them all to the same warm friendliness. Myra Dougal might think her soft in the head, but then Myra rarely had to bring in her Vacancies sign.

Dusk was casting long shadows across the lane as Win glanced out of her kitchen window for the tenth time in as many minutes. Katie's stay had extended past the weekend, and she'd eventually confided in Win that she'd taken a week's leave, and might yet make it a fortnight. Each morning she pulled on her walking boots and headed out of the village, not returning to the guesthouse until late in the afternoon. Win turned towards her husband. Crackling snapped and the air filled with the rich aroma of succulent meat as he began to carve thick slices of roast pork from a joint not long out of the oven. "Do you think we should call someone?"

"She's barely ten minutes late for dinner." Jonathan stabbed at a succulent slice of meat and transferred it to the last of the seven plates on the table before him.

"Yes, but a young woman walking on the hills alone, anything could've happened to her." Win snapped off the gas as a saucepan of peas threatened to boil over. "And here we are, calmly serving up dinner as though everything is just hunky dory."

"Well, one of us is calm," he observed, as she strained the saucepan while looking out of the window. Several peas made a break for freedom.

"I'm just saying…" She stopped abruptly. Was that the front door? She shoved the saucepan onto the draining board and then hurried into the hallway. Thank goodness. Katie was in the porch, bending down as she tugged at the knotted laces of her walking boots.

"Sorry I'm late." She glanced up, peering through a curtain of wind-tangled blonde hair. "It took longer than I expected to get back from the crag."

"You look tired." The urge to indulge in a maternal scolding died at the sight of her. The girl needed to walk less and sleep more.

Katie straightened up, and then glanced towards the dining room. Laughter spilled into the hallway; a middle-aged couple and their three teenagers were recounting their day's adventure to one another. Was that hesitation on Katie's face?

"If you want to shower and change before dinner we can keep your plate warm," Win offered.

Katie shook her head. "I don't want to put you to any more trouble. Besides, I'd hate to miss Jonathan's dinnertime tale. It's the highlight of the day. Everyone says so."

Win snorted, hiding her pride in her husband. "Don't encourage him. He'll be wanting his own TV show next." The comment made Katie smile. That was better. She was far too sombre most of the time. "In you go then. There's bread on the table. Baked it myself. Dinner will be right through."

Win hurried back to the kitchen. "Something is haunting that child."

"She's hardly a child," Jonathan protested. "She must be twenty-five if she's a day."

"It doesn't matter how old she is," Win said, mashing potatoes with more force than was necessary. "She's not here just to enjoy the fresh air. You mark my words."

"Win, love," Jonathan began.

"I know. I know. We're running a bed and breakfast not a counselling service."

"Exactly."

"Nothing wrong with offering a listening ear, though, is there?" She pulled a face at him as he gave a long-suffering sigh. "Are those plates ready?"

"Aye." Taking one in each hand, he headed for the dining room.

Win hurriedly transferred the peas and potatoes to serving dishes, and then followed him. As she joined in Jonathan's banter with the guests, she was conscious of Katie intently observing all that they did as usual. She was like the audience of a TV reality show, fascinated by the mundane. Very strange. Why would a young woman find a middle-aged couple so fascinating? And why was she holidaying alone?

"I said I'm fine."

Katie's voice reached Win as she climbed the basement stairs. Her arms full of clean, freshly folded sheets from the tumble dryer below, she froze at the exasperation of Katie's tone. For a moment she couldn't imagine who she was talking to. Jonathan was in the garden, picking vegetables for dinner, and all their other guests had gone out for the day.

Reaching the top of the stairs, she peered down the hallway. Katie was standing by the front door, her back to Win, one hand hidden beneath her hair by her right ear. Oh, a mobile phone. Of course. Kids these days never went far without one. Not wanting to eavesdrop she hurried into the kitchen.

"Don't be silly, Jed. The last thing I want to do is hurt you."

33

Oh dear. She could still hear every word. She moved towards the door, intending to close it.

"No," Katie said. "I'm not telling you where I am." Win's hand froze on the doorknob. "You know why, so please, don't keep asking."

Ah, proof. Katie was in trouble of some kind. Vindication was quickly replaced by fresh concern.

"Win?" Jonathan's voice sounded from behind her. "What are you doing?"

She pushed the door shut, and spun round, trying not to look guilty. Jonathan was standing in the frame of the outside door, a large cabbage in one hand and a bucket of earthy potatoes in the other. "Don't you bring those muddy boots in here, Jonathan Farnham," she scolded, gesturing at his dirty Wellingtons.

"What were you doing?" he asked, setting the vegetables down, and sitting on the doorstep, his back to her as he began to tug at his boots.

"When?" she asked feigning innocence. "Cup of tea?"

"Just now. And yes, a cup of tea would be lovely." He twisted round, eyebrows raised in question.

She huffed out a breath, not wanting to lie. Besides, he knew her far too well for her to get away with it. "If you must know, Katie was talking to someone on her mobile telephone. I didn't intend to listen in, but it was rather difficult given she was right in the hallway." She flipped the switch on the kettle, and turned to face him. "Sounds like she's hiding from someone."

"That really isn't our business." Jonathan padded barefoot to the sink, and then tipped a generous amount of potatoes into the bowl.

"What if it was Maddy? If our daughter was in the kind of trouble that made her run away and stay with strangers, you'd want them looking out for her, wouldn't you?"

"Well yes, of course I would." Jonathan turned the tap on. He glanced over his shoulder at her. "Let me guess, you have a plan."

Win moved behind him, wrapped her arms around his waist and pressed her face into the curve between his shoulder blades. He smelt like the garden after a shower of rain – a comforting mix of damp soil and fresh green leaves. She allowed herself a brief moment to savour his strength, his solidity, and the fact that she'd never had a conversation with him like the one Katie had just had with the mysterious Jed. "Yes," she said. "I have a plan."

Thursday was often a day of calm, and this week was no exception. Apart from Katie, the guesthouse was empty, new arrivals not expected until Friday evening. Usually Win and Jonathan would make the most of the quiet – driving into the city to see a play or to enjoy a meal they hadn't had to prepare. This evening, though, Win had plans of a different kind.

"Are you sure about this?" Jonathan asked as he pulled on his jacket.

"Trust me," Win replied. "Besides, we both know you've been itching to spend an evening with Fred Davis and that wreck of a car."

"Don't let Fred hear you call his classic MG a wreck." Clearly relishing the idea of playing with oil filters and brake pads, he smiled and kissed her cheek. "I'll be home about eleven."

As the door closed behind him, Win swung into action. Nothing was quite like homemade food: shepherd's pie, apple crumble. It was comfort for the stomach and the soul. Just before seven o'clock she heard the front door open. Quickly she darted into the hallway, smiling at Katie who was hanging a damp waterproof jacket on the coat stand.

"It's just the two of us this evening," she said casually. "I wondered if you'd like to join me in the kitchen for dinner. Seems a bit daft you sitting all alone in the dining room, and me out there on my own."

"Oh." Katie looked momentarily startled, but then politeness won out. "I'd like that. Thanks."

Ten minutes later the two women were seated at the kitchen table. Win kept the conversation light and non-threatening. TV programmes. Favourite books. It wasn't until Katie declared she couldn't possibly eat another mouthful that Win casually asked, "Would it help if you talked about it?"

"About what?" Puzzlement drew Katie's brows together.

"Whatever it is you're running away from." Blunt and to the point. It usually worked, especially when someone had been softened with good food. "I only ask because you seem like you could use a friend."

Katie stared at her for a long moment, then huffed out a breath. Her gaze slid to the Welsh dresser with its jumble of family photographs. "How long have you and Mr Farnham been married?"

Okay, so she didn't want to talk about it. Win swallowed her disappointment. "Thirty-four years. Thirty-five come the spring."

"Thirty-five years," Katie repeated, a hint of awe in her tone. She traced a figure of eight with her spoon in the remains of the custard in her bowl. "How have you managed to stay together so long?"

Win raised her eyebrows, offended that this young woman should think her such an ill-fit to Jonathan.

Colour raced into Katie's cheeks as she looked up. "Oh no, Win, I didn't mean to imply... No, no, please, that was not my intent. I really admire you, both of you. I merely meant to ask how you – how anyone made a marriage work for so many years." She sighed heavily. "My family has a very poor track record when it comes to marriage."

36

"I see," Win said, considering the question. "Well, we talk a lot."

Katie laughed. "I'd noticed that. Jonathan does love to tell a story, doesn't he?"

"Aye, but it's more than just story telling. We talk about everything. The good and the bad. It's kept us close." She paused, not wanting to get involved in a Good Marriage seminar. "Look, Katie, I don't mean to interfere, but I couldn't help but overhear your conversation this morning."

"Oh." Katie stared down at her bowl.

"Like I said, if you need a friend or, well, you know." Win reached out and gently squeezed Katie's arm. Katie didn't move. Didn't look up. Oh well, she'd made the offer. Wasn't much more she could do. "Tea?" she asked. Her chair scraped noisily across the tiles as she pushed herself away from the table. Katie nodded. Win busied herself with the kettle and mugs. Oh dear. She was a fool. Katie was young and probably had loads of friends to confide in. No doubt she thought her an old busybody.

"Sugar?" Win asked, turning. The kitchen table was deserted. She spun round, and saw Katie standing by the Welsh dresser, staring at the photographs. Thank goodness. For a moment, she'd thought Katie had simply run for her room.

"No. Thank you." Katie picked up a sun-faded wedding photograph. Win instantly knew which photo; herself in a pretty Laura Ashley dress, Jonathan with hair almost as long as her own.

Katie exhaled a long breath as though exhausted. "He asked me to marry him."

Milk jug in hand, Win froze. What? Who? Her brain refused to connect the dots.

"Jed," Katie said. "My boyfriend. The guy on the phone." She set the photo back in its place, and folded her arms over her chest, hugging herself. "We've only been together two months. We hardly know each other."

Win gave a soft laugh. "You can be with someone thirty-five years, my dear, and they'll still find ways to surprise you."

"I didn't know what to say," Katie continued. "I didn't even know what to think. Strange really. I'm the one that's always being accused of being impulsive, but when he mentioned marriage – I needed to get away. Needed somewhere to think. And so I came here."

"Which was impulsive in its own way," Win observed. She paused and then gently asked, "Do you love him?"

"I think so."

"Think so?"

"I keep trying to imagine what life would be like without him and, well, I don't think I could bear it. So I guess that means I love him."

"I'd say that was a pretty good clue," Win agreed.

"And it isn't that I don't want to be with him or spend the rest of my life with him, it's just – "

"Just what?" Win prompted.

"I'm afraid," Katie admitted. "My parents split up when I was young. It was horrible. All the shouting, the hurt, the anger. It got really ugly – fights over money, fights over me." She grimaced. "Eventually Dad said he'd had enough and he moved up this way. I only saw him at weekends. We'd walk on the hills and talk and…" She stopped. "I don't want to go through that, all that my parents went through."

Win wanted to say that history doesn't always repeat itself, but it seemed trite. And besides, she read the papers. She knew how many marriages ended in divorce. What could she say? What reassurance could she possibly give?

"Thing is," Katie said. "I'm afraid that if I say no, if I tell Jed I don't want to get married, I'll lose him, that he won't understand. His family is big on marriage. Dead opposite of mine. He believes in it all – church ceremony, honeymoon, a couple of kids and the whole happy ever after thing." She sipped at her tea. "I want to believe in it

38

too. Really I do." She looked at Win. "Being here, seeing you and Jonathan, it's made me think that maybe, just maybe it is possible. It is, isn't it? Marriages can work, can't they?"

Win smiled as she thought of Jonathan. "Yes, my dear, they can. But you've said the right word – work."

Katie frowned. "What do you mean?"

"You like walking, right? Think of marriage like a path. Sometimes it's very steep and rocky and you can hardly figure out the way ahead. At other times it's like a stroll along a river bank on a summer's day." She finished making the tea and carried a mug over to Katie. "Sometimes it takes work."

"But there's no guarantee we'll make it through the rocky parts," Katie said quietly, as she took her tea.

"No, but is that a reason to not set out on the path at all?"

Katie didn't answer. Not knowing what else to say, Win changed the subject.

"Mrs Tanner would like scrambled eggs on toast, and her husband wants a full English," Win said, aiming the order at Jonathan who was busy with the frying pan. She turned towards the toaster. Two slices of brown for the Carpenters. Three slices of white for the Alwins. Or was it three white and two brown? She sighed, and shoved three of each into the slots. She needed to focus, to look after her guests, and to top fretting about Katie.

The kettle clicked off. She made a pot of tea, and then carried it into the dining room. The empty place at the table mocked her. Katie had gone out at the crack of dawn. Worse, Jonathan had found a note by the telephone informing them that she wouldn't need her room that night. She was leaving. Returning only to pick up her stuff and pay her bill.

Janet Alder was watching her, concern on her face. "Everything all right, Win?"

Smile. Play the perfect hostess. "Aye, right as rain."
No. No. She'd tried to help.

And failed.

The day crawled from breakfast to lunch to afternoon tea. Win kept busy. It wasn't difficult. There was always something to clean or dust. Four o'clock found her polishing furniture in the sitting room. Jonathan was reading the local newspaper and muttering about the new supermarket the nearby town had just approved. They both looked up at the sound of the front door opening.

"Win? Jonathan?"

It was Katie's voice. Win twisted her duster into a contorted sausage. "In here, my dear."

Katie appeared in the doorway. She was wearing a blue t-shirt, jeans, and trainers. "Did you get my note?"

"Aye."

"Good. I didn't want you to turn anyone away because you thought you were full."

"That was very thoughtful, my dear, but like I said before, I don't normally let that room."

"Right. Of course." Katie smiled. "Anyway, there's someone I want you to meet." She turned, beckoned to an unseen figure in the hallway, and then stepped into the room. "This is Jed. I caught the first bus into town so I could meet him at the railway station."

"Jed?" Win stared at the young man. Jed? The voice on the end of the phone? Want-to-be-fiancé Jed?

"We have some news," Katie said, her smile even brighter now. "I want you to be the first to know." She took a deep breath, grinned at Jed, and then at Win. "We're getting married. First week in December, if we can find somewhere to have the service."

Married? It took a moment to sink in. "That's wonderful!" Win dropped the mangled duster and crossed the room to give Katie a hug. "Congratulations." And to think she'd been so worried, had berated herself over and over for interfering.

Jonathan was on his feet now, shaking Jed's hand. "I presume we can trust you to take good care of her," he said.

"Jonathan," Win protested. "You're not the father of the bride."

Jonathan snorted. "Lass has been under my roof for nigh on a week. That gives me certain responsibilities."

"It's okay, Mrs Farnham," Jed said quickly. "Yes, Mr Farnham. I intend to take very good care of her."

"You will come to the wedding, won't you?" Katie asked. "Both of you?" She gave Win a shy smile. "It wouldn't do for us to get married without our role models there."

"Role models?" Win asked.

"Katie says you and Mr Farnham have been married for thirty-five years," Jed said with admiration in his tone. "That's quite something." He slipped his arm around Katie's shoulders, his affection obvious. "Thanks to you two, she's willing to take a chance on us."

Win looked at Jonathan. Role model, story teller, and her partner for life. A warm glow settled around her, and she looked back at the newly engaged couple. "Oh no, my dears, thirty-five years is nothing. We're only just getting out of the honeymoon stage. Isn't that right, darling?"

Jonathan laughed and kissed her forehead. "Absolutely." He drew in a deep breath. "Why don't we celebrate with a nice cup of tea? And I'll tell you the tale of how we got engaged."

## Chalk and Cheese

Well, so much for being mature. First sign of trouble and what had she done? Run off like a cowardy custard, that's what.

Abigail kicked at a piece of flint as she walked along the beach. Cowardy custard, she accused herself again. The childish words were more than appropriate. Running away at her age was ridiculous. She was a married woman now and far too old to be doing such things.

Married – tears threatened at that thought. She thrust her hands deep into the pockets of her fleece jacket and peered out to sea. Blinking hard she tried to pretend it was the sting of the wind causing the dampness on her cheeks. *Oh Tom, why did you have to go and spoil everything?*

A seagull flew overhead, squawking angrily at another bird that had stolen a choice morsel of bread. I know how you feel, Abigail told the gull silently. Happy one minute, devastated the next. *Oh, dear God, help me do the right thing.*

Now look, she was praying and she wasn't sure she even believed in God. Next she'd be talking to plants.

She turned away, intent on following the curve of the beach towards the pier. She needed to walk – it was always so much easier to think things through calmly and rationally when she had the scrunch of beach pebbles beneath her feet and fresh salt-scented air in her lungs.

She took five steps and then froze. *Oh no.* Surely that couldn't be her mother. She squinted at the woman on the seawall. Duffle-coat, blue scarf, sensible shoes: there was no doubt about it. That was definitely her mother. Now she really did feel like a child. She shot the clouds a sour look. This was hardly the answer to prayer she might have hoped for.

"Abigail?" Her mother was waving now.

There was nothing for it but to wave back. Dismayed, she watched her mother hurry down the steps to the beach. The last thing she wanted was company. A curl of hair had escaped her ponytail; irritated she tucked it firmly behind one ear and tried to act as though there was nothing unusual about being found miles from home, walking alone on a windswept beach. "Hello, Mum."

"What on earth are you doing here, Abi? Tom is worried sick."

Guilt caught at her. "He called you?"

"Of course he called me. Do you think I'd be down here on a freezing cold afternoon if he hadn't?"

Abigail frowned. "But how did you know I was here? I didn't tell Tom where I was going."

Her mother's face softened. "I still have memories of those moody teenage days when you used to flounce out of the house and head down here."

*Great, she'd reverted to form.* Abigail gave a rueful smile. "I guess you know me better than I know myself then. When I got in the car I had no idea where I was going. I just wanted to get away on my own for awhile."

"You should call him, Abi. Let him know you're okay."

"Yes, I will," Abigail said, fighting another rush of guilt. *Just, not right now. Not yet.* She tensed, waiting for the inevitable interrogation.

To her surprise, her mother merely gazed out at the horizon, wrapping her scarf around her neck. "It is beautiful down here – cold, though. Shall we walk for a bit?"

"Aren't you going to give me the third degree?" Abigail asked, surprised.

Her mother glanced at her, and then looked away. "I think you're a bit old for that, don't you?" She gestured towards the pier. "Shall we?"

Stunned, Abigail fell in step beside her and for several long moments the only sounds were those of the waves and the wind.

"Tom's been offered a job in America," Abigail blurted out, her mother's silence finally getting to her.

Her mother kept walking. "Yes, I know."

"Told you about it, did he?"

"Yes."

"Did he also tell you that he accepted it without so much as taking a moment to think about what it means for me?" Abigail felt her temper spark again.

Her mother glanced at her. "Ah, I take it that's why you're angry with him?"

"Too right, although I don't suppose I should be surprised that he rushed head long into this," Abigail continued. "And neither should you. After all, you were the one who warned me he was the impetuous type, and that this wasn't necessarily a good thing."

Her mother nodded, unabashed. "Well you had only known each other a couple of weeks when you came home sporting an engagement ring. It did seem a rather hasty decision."

"Yes, well, apparently Tom's impulsiveness wasn't a one off. I'm beginning to realise this is how he lives life. Snap decisions – they come to him as easily as drawing breath." Decisions that threw things into turmoil, she thought bitterly.

Her fingers found a tissue in her pocket. She pulled it out, blew her nose loudly, determined not to cry in front of her mother.

"You should've seen him, Mum. He came through the door like a kid on Christmas morning who had just been given a shiny new toy." She sighed. "I feel like we've barely finished unwrapping our wedding presents, and now he wants me to pack everything up and move half way round the world with him."

"Well," her mother said slowly. "If you really love him…"

"Of course I love him," Abigail snapped. "And when he started telling me about the job I was so proud of him but then —" She paused, trying to keep her emotions under control. "I suddenly realised that this great opportunity of his means I have to leave everything else I love behind – my job, my friends – " She glanced at her mother. "You and Dad."

"Ah," her mother said sympathetically.

"I know I'm being selfish, but I got rather cross with him," Abigail admitted, but then confessed, "Actually I was furious with him. He kept trying to tell me that his company would help us move, that there'd be lots of support, and that I'd make new friends and find a new job, and all I could think was –" She paused, exhausted by the sudden rush of words and memories. "Honestly, you'd have thought he was suggesting we buy a different brand of baked beans rather than springing a move to another country on me."

"So you ran away," her mother said pointedly.

"Yes," said Abigail shamefaced. "I know I shouldn't have, that it was silly and childish, but I needed some time to think – about the job, the move, about me and Tom and whether we actually have a future together."

Her mother looked shocked. "Oh Abi, surely you're not thinking of leaving Tom for good."

"But don't you see, he's the one doing the leaving. He's the one who's taken a job a thousand miles away!" Frustrated she kicked at a pebble. It flew up in the air and then landed with a sharp crack – a very odd sounding crack.

"Did you hear that?" Abigail asked, peering across the tumble of stones.

"Sounded like something breaking," her mother said.

Abigail was already striding along the trajectory the stone had taken. "Oh my goodness, look at this." Lying on the pebbles were two pieces of pure white chalk, each shaped like half an apple. Abigail scooped them up. "Incredible, they fit together, look." She held the two halves together, showing her mother how they formed a perfect sphere. "That stone I kicked, it must've hit the chalk in just the right place to split it in two."

Guilt and loss washed over Abigail. She'd done this; it was her anger that had split the chalk. She stared down at the stones beneath her feet. Sharp, angular flints jostled for space amongst the weather-smoothed cobbles and pebbles. Browns, whites and greys, the colours merged into a tapestry that spoke of wind and rain, storms and sunshine. Nothing fitted together as snugly as the two halves of chalk in her hand, and now it was spoilt. If she put them back on the beach the wind and the rain would swiftly erode them and they would never fit together again. She couldn't let that happen. It didn't feel right.

"Let no man tear apart that which God has joined," she said softly, recalling the words of the marriage service.

"What made you say that?" her mother asked, puzzled.

"The way the chalk split in two," Abbey said. "It just made me think – I know it sounds silly, but it almost seems like some kind of sign." She hesitated and then added slowly. "Or perhaps some kind of warning."

A shiver ran down Abigail's back as she suddenly had the strangest feeling that she and her mother weren't alone on the beach. She glanced round, but there was no one else – no living thing save for a lone seagull standing just out of reach of the surf. Her gaze turned inland, towards the sea front with its rainbow-coloured row of beach huts. She smiled as she saw something familiar.

"See that seat?" she said.

"The one by the Victorian lamp post?"

Abigail nodded. "Tom and I had a picnic sitting right there a couple of months ago."

"You did?" Her mother frowned, clearly trying to place the event in her mind.

"You didn't know about it," Abigail said. "I'd casually mentioned how much I missed the beach and the sea to Tom during the week, and that Friday he picked me up from work and drove me here. He'd packed a picnic – my favourite cheese, bread from that bakery round the corner from our flat, two chocolate muffins that he'd made himself. By the way, he bakes muffins that rival yours."

Her mother smiled. "Actually, he called me for the recipe."

"He did?" Abigail stared at her mother in surprise.

"Yes, completely out of the blue. Like you say, he can be impulsive."

"Yes." Abigail smiled, remembering the taste of chocolate, the sound of the waves singing gently, the warmth of Tom's arm around her shoulders. *Oh God, what was she doing here?*

"You drove all this way and didn't drop in?" Her mother sounded disappointed.

"I suggested it, but he didn't want to put you to any trouble at such short notice. Besides, he'd booked us into a bed and breakfast just down the coast. As well as the picnic he'd packed an overnight bag for the two of us."

"That was thoughtful of him. He must love you a great deal."

"Yes." Abigail ran her thumb against the smooth surface of the chalk. She didn't doubt that he loved her and wanted her to be happy.

She pressed the two flat chalk surfaces together again, and then pulled the elastic scrunchie from her ponytail. The wind whipped her hair across her face, but she ignored the sting. Carefully she stretched the elastic over the sphere so it held the two halves together. "If I tied a piece of ribbon around this, it would make a nice decoration, don't you think?"

"I suppose so," her mother said doubtfully. "Where would you put it?"

"Oh, somewhere on display at home." She paused and then added softly. "Wherever home might end up being."

She held the chalk ball up to the fading sun. "Two have become one," she said, remembering her wedding day. She glanced at her mother. "I know you think I rushed into marrying him, but I really do love him."

"I never doubted that you did, Abi."

"No, but you didn't think I'd thought things through enough, and maybe you were right." Marrying Tom had been so exciting – the planning, the ceremony, the honeymoon, all of it. But now, she suddenly realised how much she actually wanted to be with him, his partner for life, how much they actually belonged together. "I made promises to Tom – for better, for worse, for richer, for poorer and all that – I intend to keep those promises." She sighed again. "I do need to talk to him though. I need to make him understand how I feel."

Her mother smiled. "That sounds like a good idea to me."

Abigail nodded. "Yes, I need him to understand that the thought of leaving everything I know is kind of scary. And he needs to know that sometimes it is great to be impetuous – like the surprise picnic – but sometimes we need to talk before we make decisions."

"Especially big ones like moving to America," her mother said, nodding.

"Yes, especially decisions like that."

"Mind you," her mother said, "there is a little bit of the pot calling the kettle black, don't you think?"

Abigail shot her surprised look, but then sucked in a deep breath, realising that perhaps it was time she reined in her own impetuous habits. "You're right. From now on, no more running away when things are difficult." She leaned forward and hugged her mother. "I think it's time I went home."

"Me too. Your father will be wondering where I've got too."

"You didn't tell him where you were going?" Abigail asked in surprise.

"I'm afraid when it comes to your well-being sometimes I can be a bit impulsive too," her mother admitted.

"Sounds like it is time we both went home to our husbands," she said. She linked her arm through her mother's and they began to make their way back towards the sea wall.

As Abigail reached the bottom of the steps, she slipped the chalk ball into her pocket, oddly comforted by the solid weight of it. Perhaps her prayer had been answered after all. She took one last lingering look at the sea, and then she glanced up at the clouds. "Thank you," she whispered, and then turned and followed her mother.

## Cracks in the Pavement

"I'll call the council later," Emily Grant said, snapping the lid closed on her first aid kit. "That pavement's a disgrace and I'll be telling them so."

"I don't want to put you to any more trouble," Jane protested, frowning at the sticking plaster on her left knee. This was the third accident in as many days – all thanks to that news report. And now, she'd ended up in the kitchen of the one person in the village she been warned to avoid.

"What are neighbours for if not to lend a hand when needed?" Emily said, oblivious to the longing look Jane gave the doorway. "You could hardly be walking up the road dripping blood, now could you? Good job I came along when I did. Now, how about a nice cup of tea?"

"That's very kind, but…"

"You're far too pale," Emily interrupted, flicking the switch on the kettle and then pulling two mugs from a cupboard. "Perhaps it's the shock of falling. Maybe you should see a doctor just to be on the safe side?"

"No really, I'm fine. Just a bit tired. That's probably why I didn't see that crack in the paving stone." Jane looked across at her young daughter, sleeping soundly in her buggy beneath Emily's kitchen window. "Lou was up half the night." Not that it mattered since sleep had eluded her all week anyway; worry had a funny way of doing that to her.

"Must be difficult being on your own," Emily said sympathetically as she put two teabags into a small brown teapot.

Jane jerked her head round to look at her. "How did you know I'm on my own?" she asked, even though she already guessed. Life in a small village where everyone seemed to think they had a right to know your business was rather different to the big town she'd lived in before.

"The grapevine is alive and well, my dear," Emily said, confirming Jane's suspicions without a hint of embarrassment. "Not that it does to believe everything that's gossiped around here."

"I see," Jane said slowly as Emily set a mug of hot tea in front of her. Oh well, since there was no point in keeping secrets, she might as well reveal all. Besides, she needed to tell someone. "Did the grapevine tell you my husband is a soldier and that I haven't heard from him for over a month now?"

"Iraq?" Emily asked softly.

"Afghanistan." Jane buried her head in her hands. "He's probably fine, after all, it isn't unusual for him to be out of touch, but the news on the telly…"

"I'm so sorry," Emily said, sounding genuinely sympathetic.

Kate sucked in a deep breath and straightened up. *What was she doing? Blabbing all to the village gossip!* "Please, don't be. I knew what I was getting into when I married him. Anyway, I'm coping just fine so there's no need for you to be concerned." The pain of her husband's absence threatened to spill out of her. Hurriedly she filled her mouth with scalding tea so she could swallow the hurt again.

Emily frowned. "I didn't mean to imply you weren't coping, my dear. Just that you look like you could use a break."

"Yes, well, there's not much chance of that with three youngsters to look after," she said with more bitterness than she intended.

"I'd be only too happy to babysit," Emily offered tentatively. "Or perhaps to look after the little one while you go shopping or get your hair done." She patted at her perfectly styled white hair, and gave an unexpectedly coquettish smile. "Us girls need our little treats."

Jane's heart sank. The offer was both unexpected and unwelcome. She'd been warned about Emily Grant's do-gooding interference. "I couldn't put you out like that," she replied. "We hardly know each other."

"Nonsense," Emily countered. "We've been passing the time of day with each other for weeks now."

"I couldn't afford to pay you."

Emily looked affronted. "I wasn't looking for money. Fact is, I'd just be glad of the company. Since Bert passed away... Well, the days can seem long when you're on your own."

"I suppose they can," Jane agreed, trying to deny the lonely evening hours after the children were tucked into bed. She sipped at her tea as the conversation lulled, wishing it would cool faster so she could escape. Looking round, though, she was surprised at how familiar Emily's kitchen seemed. The warm yellows of the floral décor were an echo of her childhood. Her mother had kept African violets on the window sill too. That her parents must've sold them or given them away when they retired to Spain made her feel sad. It was the kind of kitchen that she wanted her kids to grow up in – homely and lived in, with their height marks notched on the doorframe and scuff marks on the skirting boards from football boots and schoolbags and... She sighed, remembering this was why she'd moved to the village instead of living with the other army wives in rented accommodation where personality was all-too-swiftly erased by a new coat of paint.

"Did you know I have wee ones of my own?" Emily asked, reaching for her handbag.

Jane shook her head. "Grandchildren?"

"Aye. Two of them." She produced a faded and creased photo. "I don't get to see much of them unfortunately – just the occasional glimpse now and again."

Jane glanced at her, wondering at the depth of sadness in her voice. Emily merely gave a wistful smile and passed the photo to her.

53

"What wonderful hair," Jane said, admiring the auburn curls of the two young children. Her own children had inherited their father's sandy-coloured hair instead of her ebony waves. She frowned as she studied the photo some more. There was something oddly familiar about the faces staring out at her. "Do they live a long way from here then?"

Emily grimaced. "I'm afraid their absence from my life is a little more complicated than that." She hesitated a moment and then said, "My daughter and I don't get on. Fact is, I think she's ashamed of me. She moves in fancy circles these days – always down the gym and off to balls and such like. And these poor children, well, seems to me they come second to her social life. Unfortunately I made the mistake of saying so to her and ever since – well, apparently I'm not the kind of grandmother she wants for her children."

"I'm sorry," Jane said, imagining how awful she would feel if she couldn't see her children. It was bad enough being apart from David for long periods.

Emily took the photo back, carefully smoothing out the crease, and then putting it back in her handbag. She straightened her back as she clipped the bag shut, her sorrow buried in its depths along with the photo. "So what do you think about my offer? You could bring the children round to play after school maybe. Let them get to know me a little first, and then if you like maybe I could play grannie? Even if you'd rather not leave them with me, it would be nice to have someone to bake for again, and you'd be doing an old lady a favour just by dropping in for a cup of tea."

"I don't know," Jane said, tempted by the idea of an hour or two to herself. "It's hard on them not having their father around. If I abandon them too… "

"Leaving them with a babysitter for an hour or two is hardly abandonment," Emily said gently.

54

"I suppose not." Jane glanced at her watch, looking for an excuse to escape without commiting herself. "Sorry, I have to go now. The boys will be out of school soon." She saw the disappointment on Emily's face, and felt guilty as it was quickly masked with a smile.

"Well, the offer's there if you wish," Emily said. "Call by any time."

It was odd that she'd never noticed how many paving stones round the estate were cracked before. Now, as she pushed Louise's buggy along the familiar paths to school, she wondered how that happened. Did the cracks slowly creep from the edges, meeting at some point predestined by the mix of sand and cement? Or did the slabs suddenly snap – cracking violently apart as the stress of being part of a pavement became too much of them.

The thought made her grimace. Was that how it would happen with her? The stress of being a single parent, of not knowing whether David was dead or alive, would it suddenly all become too much and she'd simply crack?

She arrived at the school gate and saw Kate Turner's gaze go straight to the plaster on her knee. Kate was, as always, immaculately groomed. Jane couldn't imagine her ever doing anything as inelegant as falling over in the street.

"What's happened now?" Kate asked.

Jane winced. "I tripped over a broken paving stone. Ended up in Emily Grant's kitchen being patched up like school kid."

Kate snorted. "Laying traps for people is she? Well, I did warn you."

Jane shook her head, suddenly uncomfortable with Kate's acidic attack on someone who had shown her kindness. "I wouldn't describe her that way. She just seemed kind of lonely to me. She offered to babysit Lou if ever I needed anyone."

"Really? From what I know of her I'd have thought she'd be more likely to report you to social services for wanting to go out."

"Maybe the gossips in this town should find something better to do with their time," Jane said tartly.

"Hey, I'm just trying to protect you from the old busybody," Kate said. "Don't be so touchy."

"Sorry. It's been a bad day." Jane changed the subject. Kate was one of the few potential friends she had in the village. She really didn't want to squabble with her. "So, talking of my non-existent social life - what are you doing tonight? Fancy coming round for a glass of wine? We could rent a movie."

"Love to," Kate said, "but I'm going to some fancy works do of Simon's. Goodness knows how I'm going to be ready in time what with Rachel's dance class and then getting them tea. Honestly, kids are such a nuisance sometimes, aren't they?"

"Tomorrow then?" Emily asked, thinking that actually tea-time with her children was one of the pleasures of her day.

"Aerobics," Kate said apologetically. "I really can't miss that. We're off on hols in a couple of weeks and I've bought a ridiculously tiny bikini." She was already moving away, beckoning to her daughter who had stepped out of her classroom. "Perhaps some time next week?"

"Sure." Jane tried not to mind that she wasn't high on Kate's list of priorities.

"Hi, Jane." Rachel ran over, her auburn curls like a halo around her head.

"Hello, Rachel, how was school today?" Jane asked, suddenly reminded of two young children in a faded photograph.

"Okay." She turned to her mother. "Sarah's having a party next Tuesday. Can I go? Please?"

Kate rolled her eyes. "I'll have to check my diary. You know how busy I am, darling."

Jane's gaze moved from Rachel's curls to Kate's face. It was hard to believe the connection her mind was making, and yet the evidence was right in front of her, impossible to deny. "Are you… " she began, too astonished to consider whether the question might be welcome.

"Not now, Jane," Kate said dismissively. "I really must dash. Come along, Rachel, you're going to make me late for my hair appointment."

Jane stared in amazement as mother and daughter hurried away. Kate was Emily Grant's daughter! She was sure of it, not just because of Rachel's hair, but because of the family resemblance in Kate's features. No wonder Kate had warned her away from Emily; she was frightened her mother would turn the spotlight on her. She felt dizzy at the realisation. Not only that, but it suddenly hit home that Kate would never be the friend that she had hoped for. Emily was right, Kate's interests focused entirely on herself.

A loud crack at Jane's feet made her jump. Shaken, she looked down and saw a clean, fresh fracture running across the paving stone she was standing on. Surely it hadn't just split beneath her? Then she heard laughter behind her and smelt the acrid scent of a firecracker. Spinning round, she saw two lads running away.

"Did you see her face?" one called to the other. "Looked like she thought the ground was about to give way under her feet."

"Stupid kids!" she shouted.

Heart still pounding from the sudden fright, her courage vanished. A tear escaped, tracking slowly down one cheek as she struggled to hold the rest at bay. Her gaze swept the playground, desperately wishing someone – anyone – would notice she was falling apart. She couldn't do this any more. She couldn't cope on her own, especially now the one person she'd hoped to build a friendship with had proven not to be the person she'd believed in. She was going to crack - just like the paving stone under her feet.

"Mum!" Her younger son called to her as he ran out of his classroom.

For a moment she felt sick and dizzy, but then the smile on his face gave her the spark of strength she needed to wipe the tears away. "Hey there, Sean. Good day at school?"

James, her other son joined them before Sean could answer. "Hi, Mum. What are we doing today? Can I invite a friend for tea?"

She looked at her two boys and marvelled at how they'd somehow managed to stay so normal, despite the absence of their father and the infrequent presence of their grandparents. Louise gurgled to herself in her buggy, grinning up at her with adoring eyes. Somehow she had to find a way to keep going, to keep being strong for them. Emily's offer came into her mind. Could the answer really be a lonely widow? Was mutual need a strong enough foundation to build a friendship on?

"Mum?" James whined impatiently.

"You can invite them to come tomorrow," she said, firmly. His face fell and she ruffled his hair with a still trembling hand. "I've got something special for us to do today."

"Oh?" The faces of both children lit up.

"I want to introduce you to a lady called Emily."

"Is she a friend of yours?" Sean asked.

Jane took a deep breath and calmed her fears. "Not yet, but I hope she might be. Let's go and find out."

Scrape, scrape, scrape – Mary Barton buttered her toasted teacake with short, sharp strokes. The new owner of the tearoom was clearly purchasing cheap cakes from the local supermarket and then passing them off as her own. The knowledge added to the sourness of Mary's mood.

"Is something wrong, Mum?" Dorothy was sitting on the other side of the table, stirring a mug of instant coffee. The aroma of freshly ground coffee beans was noticeably absent from the tearoom these days too.

"Why do people have to change everything?" Mary asked. She frowned at the plastic tablecloth that had replaced crisp white linen.

Dorothy sipped her coffee, winced, and then gave a rueful smile. "I think they call it progress." Her expression turned quizzical. "That isn't why you were punishing that teacake, though, is it. Come on, Mum, what's really bothering you?"

Mary's butter knife clattered against her plate as she set it down. She should've known her daughter would pick up on her mood. For a moment she wrestled with herself, not wanting to burden Dorothy with her problems, yet longing to have someone in whom she could confide.

"Mum?" Dorothy prompted. She moved the small glass vase with its single plastic daffodil to one side of the table as though clearing space for a heart-to-heart.

Mary sighed wearily. "It's your father."

"Oh?" Dorothy immediately looked concerned.

Guilt pricked Mary. It really wasn't fair to share her worries with her daughter, but if she didn't tell someone… She glanced at the other customers, and then leaned forward. She kept her voice low, speaking in little more than a hissed whisper. "He's taken to sneaking out of the house."

"Sneaking?" Dorothy's expression changed to one of puzzled surprise.

"There's no other word for it. One minute he's sitting in the armchair reading the paper, and then, poof, he's sneaking off down the garden path without so much as a word to me."

"He doesn't tell you where he's going?" Disapproval edged Dorothy's tone.

"Not to my face, no. Sometimes he leaves a note in the kitchen or he'll send me one of those text things on that mobile phone you gave me at Christmas. Never any details, of course, just some vague comment about having some errands to run. I ask you, what errands can he possibly have that require him to sneak off without so much as a word?"

"Well…" Dorothy considered for a moment, and then shrugged, clearly bemused. "I have no idea. What does he say when he comes home?"

Mary frowned. "Nothing, and if I try to ask he just says he was doing 'this and that'." She snorted. "What sort of an answer is 'this and that?'" Her fingers worried at a currant. There were only three in the teacake. It was a disgrace.

Dorothy was studying her with concern. "Mum…" she said slowly, clearly reluctant to voice her thoughts. "Are you trying to tell me Dad's having an affair?"

A stab of anguish shot through Mary, but she gave a snort of laughter as though the suggestion was the most preposterous thing she'd ever heard. "Of course not. This is your father we're talking about." The words sounded hollow, but the act seemed to convince Dorothy.

"Good point." Dorothy nodded her agreement. "He is seventy-eight, after all."

Indignation flared at that, and she gave Dorothy a sharp look. "I suppose you think we're far too old to be troubled by affairs of the heart."

60

"Of course, not." Dorothy had the grace to look repentant. "It's just that you're celebrating your emerald wedding anniversary in a couple of weeks. Fifty-five years of marriage, and Dad's never so much as looked at another woman, right?"

"Not to my knowledge." She'd always been rather proud of the fact. Now though, she couldn't help but wonder if the old adage wasn't true, and that pride did indeed come before a fall.

Dorothy was looking at her with fond amusement. "There you go then. Whatever he's up to, it's not that."

Behind Dorothy was a display of tearoom goodies – frosted carrot cake, dark chocolate sponge, Viennese fingers. Mary felt slightly nauseous at the sight. She focused on Dorothy's face once more, wishing she could believe her daughter was right.

Dorothy sighed heavily. "Okay, what haven't you told me?"

"You'll think me crazy."

"Quite possibly, but tell me anyway."

"I think somebody is trying to seduce your father with cakes." There, she'd voiced the silly thing that had been gnawing away at her for days now. She studied Dorothy, looking for reassurance that the idea was as absurd as she hoped it was.

Dorothy blinked in surprised. "Cakes?" She repeated the word slowly, as though she hadn't heard correctly.

"He's always had a sweet tooth. Everyone knows that."

"Well, yes, but what on earth makes you think he's being tempted away by cakes?"

Mary glanced furtively at the other customers in the tearoom. It wouldn't do for anyone she knew to overhear this conversation. People could be such gossips, and this was mortifying enough without every Tom, Dick and Harry talking about it. She lowered her voice again. "He's been coming home with white smudges on his jacket. It's icing sugar. I tasted it to be sure."

"Icing sugar?" Dorothy rested her elbows on the table and rubbed at her temples.

Mary tutted, the sound more wearied than annoyed. "Darling, do try not to parrot everything I say."

"Sorry, it's just…"

"Yes, yes, I know how ridiculous it sounds, but I've been trying to convince myself I'm worrying about nothing, but…" She hesitated, not wanting to give the words weight by speaking them. It couldn't be avoided, though. "Last Thursday I saw him coming out of Irene Hewitt's."

Dorothy shook her head, disbelief on her face. "You surely don't suspect Irene. You two have been friends for years. She wouldn't do that to you, and Dad certainly wouldn't. Maybe he was just helping her out with something. You know how he likes to be useful."

If only she could believe that, then everything would be right with the world again. She took a deep breath and tossed out the last piece of damning evidence. "That was the morning he had a pink smudge on his face."

"Jam?" Dorothy asked, her tone edged with desperation.

"Irene wears a rose-coloured lipstick when she's trying to make an impression." Mary frowned, recalling the sight. It hadn't really looked like lipstick, but what else could it possibly be?

Dorothy raised her hands as though facing a loaded gun. "Mum, this is insane. I really can't believe Dad is having an affair with Mrs Hewitt or anyone else for that matter."

"Well neither can I, but what other explanation can there be?"

Dorothy considered for a moment. "Have you asked him about it?"

Mary shook her head. How could she even begin to tackle such a thing? Her best friend and her husband? Perhaps it was better not to know.

Dorothy leaned forward, her expression earnest. "Well I think you should. There's probably a perfectly logical explanation. Maybe he just popped in to help her with a dripping tap or something. And maybe she just happened to have been baking."

"She's a wonderful cook. Everyone knows that."

"Yes, but that hardly puts her on the same footing as the wicked witch tempting Hansel and Gretel into the forest with gingerbread."

"I suppose not."

Dorothy sighed. "Would you like me to talk to Dad?"

Mary shook her head. "No, dear. If anyone is going to confront him, it should be me."

Dorothy reached across the table and squeezed her mother's hand. "I bet you there's nothing sinister going on at all."

Mary smiled weakly. Dorothy was no doubt right. There would be a perfectly logical explanation for Bert's strange behaviour, and she'd discover these silly little worries were about nothing at all. After all, they had enjoyed fifty-five good years of marriage. She loved him, and he loved her, and that was a fact.

She glanced round the tearoom, noticing the bright new posters that had replaced the faded watercolours. Unease sent a shiver down her spine. The problem was that things did change whether you wanted them to or not. That was a fact too.

Mary dished a generous helping of shepherd's pie onto Bert's plate. It was one of his favourite meals. Plain, simple food was what Bert liked. Plain, simple food and a slice of cake. She sighed heavily as she added peas and carrots to the plate. *Just ask him about it.* It was sure to be just as Dorothy had said, that he was helping Irene with a leaking tap or sorting out her video player or some such. Bert wouldn't do anything to hurt her. Dorothy was right, they'd been together far too long for things to go wrong now.

Right, she'd ask him what he was up to, and then it would all be sorted. No more silly worries. She'd probably even laugh at her own foolishness. Newly determined, she carried the plates into the dining room and set them on the table.

"Thanks, love." Bert put down the newspaper, picked up his fork and shovelled meat and potato into his mouth. "Delicious as always."

She speared a piece of carrot, chewed it slowly and then looked across the table at her husband. *Okay, take a deep breath and ask.* "Did I see you coming out of Irene's the other afternoon?"

His hand froze midway between his plate and his mouth. Gravy dripped from his fork. For a moment he looked startled, but then he shrugged. "Irene's? Didn't I mention I'd popped in there?"

She tried to appear nonchalant. "Must've slipped your mind." The fork continued its journey, and she watched him chew, then swallow. "Odd that she hasn't mentioned you popping in either, though."

He met her gaze calmly. "She had a couple of tiles come loose in her kitchen. Not exactly exciting news, love. I fixed them back on for her – bit of grout and everything was right as rain."

"Mix the grout yourself, did you?"

He looked puzzled, but then nodded. "Yes."

"Right, that'll explain the white powder on your jacket the other day then."

"Guess it does." He forked up more pie, and then smiled. "This is really good, love. Did you add something different?"

She stared at him for a long moment, trying to calm the sudden churning of her stomach. "Must be the gravy granules," she finally managed to say. "I think the company has changed the recipe."

He nodded cheerfully. "Everything changes sooner or later, I guess."

"Yes." Everything did. Including her husband, who had just lied to her for the first time in fifty-five years of marriage.

Saturday should've been one of the happiest days of her life. Instead, Mary dressed with a heavy heart. Across the room, Bert was standing in front of the mirrored wardrobe door, buttoning up his jacket. He'd been a handsome young man, and while the years had thinned his hair and added lines to his face, she still thought him as dashing as ever.

He saw her looking and smiled at her reflection. "You look beautiful."

"Do I?" She tugged at the cuff of her champagne-coloured blouse, unconvinced.

Bert crossed the room and gently rubbed the material of her collar between his thumb and finger. "Silk, just like your wedding dress."

She laughed softly. "Not made from a parachute though." Memories flooded back; a wedding in 1950 had been a challenge thanks to post-war rationing. Clothing coupons were still in use, and many basics were still in short supply. Despite the difficulties, it had been a wonderful day, though. A wonderful day that had been followed by many happy years. She pushed her recent doubts away, and made herself smile.

Bert kissed her cheek, and then offered her his arm. "Ready?"

She nodded. "As ready as I'll ever be."

The family was waiting downstairs. Dorothy and her husband, Geoff, were sitting on the sofa, sipping tea. Her two granddaughters, Julie and Christine, were fussing with babies and toddlers. Poppy, the eldest of the great-

65

grandchildren, was using her father as a climbing frame; he didn't seem to mind in the slightest. They all turned to look as Mary and Bert stepped into the room. Dorothy smiled. "You look lovely, Mum."

"Thank you, dear." She smiled at them, grateful that they'd all come to share this special day.

"Right everyone, let's go." Dorothy began to marshal the family out of the door to the waiting cars.

Ten minutes later they arrived at the village hall. A crowd of friends were waiting by the door, and they cheered as Mary and Bert got out of the car.

"Oh my, I feel like visiting royalty," Mary said with a laugh.

"Happy anniversary," called one of their neighbours.

"Congratulations!" someone else shouted.

Mary was kept busy shaking hands and being hugged for the next few minutes. Suddenly, Irene Hewitt stepped out of the crowd.

"Happy anniversary, Mary." Irene leaned forward and kissed Mary's cheek. "I'm so very happy for you."

"Thank you." The smile on Mary's face froze as she saw Irene wink at Bert. What was that for? Her stomach twisted uneasily. There was definitely something going on between them. What more proof did she need?

Bert was by her side again. He caught her hand in his own. "Come on, love, there's something I want you to see."

Still numb from what she'd just seen, she allowed herself to be led into the village hall. Bert guided her down the narrow corridor, past the kitchen and the cloakroom. When they reached the far end he opened the doors to the main hall with a flourish.

Mary knew her granddaughters had been hard at work all morning, decorating the room for the celebration. She twisted round and gave them an appreciative smile, before turning back to admire their handiwork. Green and white ribbons were twined round the chairs. A large banner was draped along the back wall, its green and gold letters spelling out 'Happy Emerald Anniversary. The tables each had posies of creamy roses tied with green velvet ribbons. At the back of the hall was a fabulous feast of homemade pies and sandwiches; the aroma was delicious and her stomach rumbled in appreciation. It was then that she spotted the cake standing on a small table in the corner of the room.

"Oh my." She gave a small gasp of surprise, and stared at it in disbelief. It was quite the most beautiful cake she'd ever seen – three round tiers decorated with pink roses and green emeralds, all made from royal icing.

"Do you like it?" Bert was looking at her intently, his expression anxious.

"It's absolutely beautiful."

He grinned and drew her across the room so they could admire it close up. "Remember our wedding cake?" he asked mischievously.

She nodded, her eyes still on the wondrous creation in front of her. "Three tiers of cardboard and Plaster of Paris. Yes, I remember." Rationing had meant icing sugar was virtually impossible to find. The local baker had, instead, created a cake that looked fabulous, but was completely fake, except for a small fruit cake hidden beneath the top-most tier of cardboard.

Bert slipped an arm around her shoulders and squeezed her affectionately. "I was racking my brain trying to think of something to make today extra special and then I remembered. At every family wedding since ours, you've always said if there was one thing you could go back in time and change at our wedding, it would be the cake."

She laughed, embarrassed that she'd said such a thing, and amazed that he'd taken note of it.

Bert continued, "When Julie was married, you looked so wistful when you saw her wedding cake. I promised myself, then, that one day you'd have the cake you always wanted and that I would make it for you. And here it is."

"You made this?" She stared at him in disbelief.

He suddenly looked embarrassed. "I have to confess, I enlisted the help of Irene Hewitt. She's been patiently teaching me how to make roses and emeralds out of royal icing. And she very kindly let me use her kitchen so it would be a surprise. But yes, it is all my own work."

Mary began to laugh. Suddenly everything made sense. "That's why you've been coming home with icing sugar on your jacket. And why I saw you sneaking out of Irene's." She laughed harder as she realised that the pale pink roses on the cake matched the colour of Irene's lipstick.

Bert blushed. "I'm sorry I lied to you about that. I wanted this to be a surprise, and I figured if you knew I was over at Irene's, what with her being so well-known for her cake making, well…

"Oh, Bert." She shook her head, realising how very foolish she'd been. "I do love you."

"I love you too." He leaned close and kissed her. "Happy anniversary."

Mary smiled. "Happy anniversary, my love."

## Part of the Family

*Author's note: This short, short story was written for a magazine that wanted stories from an unusual point of view. Apparently this was a bit too unusual!*

They are squabbling again. Harsh words bounce off newly painted walls and pristine wooden floors. I try not to listen, but it's impossible. She doesn't want me here and she's shouting the fact loud enough for the neighbours to hear.

The tragic thing is that I really liked Emma at first. She filled the house with the scent of summer, and she sang in the shower, belting out hits by Kylie. I found it oddly comforting; the house had been silent for too long. Foolishly, I was excited about being part of a proper family again. Now I know better.

It wasn't long before the arguments began. Over the past few months I've become all too familiar with the pattern of their relationship. They bicker and argue, and then he capitulates – anything for a quiet life. There's a cost, though. He doesn't smile any more, and sometimes he seems like a stranger in his own home.

I flinch as her words buffet me. She's saying I don't fit in. The problem is she's right; I don't – not any more. Once she moved in she began to change things, fending off his protests with clever words and emotional blackmail.

Out went the old sofa with its squishy orange cushions. In came a brand new leather suite, and with it curtains and wooden flooring. The smell of paint permeated everything for weeks. When the makeover finally reached my room I tried not to mind. After all, what does it really matter whether the walls are dusky pink instead of lime-green. I even tried not to care that she obviously favours the twins over me – after all, they are hers, whereas I'm a reminder of a life she had no part of.

The sound of the bedroom door being slammed makes me jump.

"Emma, please – don't do this."

I cringe at the distress in his voice. Then I hear footsteps on the landing. She's heading my way. Heavier footsteps behind indicate he is following. The door to my room is flung open and she grabs hold of me.

"Your choice," she snaps. "One of us has to go. Which is it going to be?"

His face twists with anguish. "Em, please – you can't be serious."

"I've never been more so," she replies. "Choose, now."

I'm rigid with terror. This is it, then. He's going to choose her and I'm going to be cast out, unloved and unwanted.

"Well?" she demands.

His shoulders slump. Defeat rests on him like a weight, but suddenly he straightens. He snatches me from her, and hugs me to his chest.

She stares at him, shocked and horrified. "Joe –"

"You wanted me to choose, I've done so. I think you'd better leave now."

Her face crumples. "You're kicking me out because of that thing?"

"This is not just a *thing*," he replies, his voice cold with anger. "My parents gave it to me when I moved into my first flat. It was with me when I trekked through Nepal. It was part of my life with Louise, and was just about the only item I kept when she left."

"Yes, but –"

"I've been telling you for weeks now, Emma, your obsession with makeovers is too much. You want to change everything: my house, my clothes – my memories. I'm tired of being part of your perfect-life project. It's over." He hesitates and then adds firmly. "We're over."

She stares at him for a long moment and then shrugs angrily. "Fine. I'll go." She snatches her matching twin towels from the rail and shoots him an ugly look. "I hope the two of you will be very happy together."

"I'm sure we will," he replies, as she stalks from the bathroom. His touch is gentle as he hangs me over the towel rail. He smiles wistfully as he straightens a wrinkle in my fabric, and then he sits on the floor and waits.

Some time later the front door slams. Emma is gone. It's just the two of us again. I hope, one day, he'll find someone who will accept him as he is – a bit worn around the edges, rather like me, but with a good heart. I hope too I'll always be part of his family.

## The Good Example

"Mummy, Mummy!" Hannah called from her bedroom. "Come and look!"

"What is it, dear?" I called back, absent-mindedly.

"It's a spider. It's ever so big."

I froze at her words. My stomach began to clench itself into a tight knot and the hairs on the back of my neck prickled uncomfortably. This was the moment Paul and I had so calmly discussed.

"We don't want Hannah to grow up full of ridiculous fears, do we?" Paul had said one night after I'd described a silly incident with a worm in the garden. "If we teach her by example she'll think it perfectly natural to handle insects and things without fear."

"I know," I said. "I'm just not sure that I'd be a very good example, that's all."

"Of course you will," Paul said, oozing confidence. He eyed me suspiciously. "You don't want her to grow up like your cousin, do you? I mean, she becomes hysterical at the mere sight of a moth."

Well, no, I didn't want that, so, of course, I'd agreed with him while secretly hoping that any insect handling would be done by him. And now here I was, both hands in the washing-up bowl and disaster about to crash around me.

"I knew you wouldn't be here," I muttered miserably to my absent husband. "Why did I ever agree to this?"

"Mummy, are you coming?" Hannah called, her voice edged with impatience.

"Yes, love," I managed to say. "I'll be right there."

Well, this is it, I thought as I dried my hands unnecessarily slowly. I began walking up the stairs, hoping that if I took long enough the spider would be gone, but as I entered Hannah's bedroom my hopes were dashed. She turned and smiled at me, her young face alight with excitement.

73

"Look!" she said, pointing at the bed. "Isn't he big?"

If there is one thing my daughter is good at it is understatement. My eyes unwillingly followed the direction of her finger. There, in the very centre of her pale yellow pillow-case was the most enormous spider I had ever seen. I stood still, overcome by the sight of its black, hairy legs.

Hannah was watching me curiously, clearly wondering why her mother had suddenly decided to make like a statue. I had to be brave. With enormous effort I moved a step nearer. The spider stared at me and waved a front leg, warning me off. I froze again, pretending I didn't want to scare it away and hoping that Hannah wouldn't realise that I was the one that was terrified.

"Are you going to pick it up, Mummy?" Hannah asked, eyeing me with the type of look she normally reserved for her heroes. The last people to be rewarded with that gaze had been Torvill and Dean as they swept majestically around the ice before scoring perfect tens. Right now I was about to score a big fat zero.

"Yes, dear," I said, trying to convince myself that this was the case. My gaze was fixed on the evil arachnid that was obviously mocking my lack of backbone. "I'm just being careful because I don't want it to run under the bed."

That at least was true. The idea of a giant spider lurking in the darkness of the bedroom was even more distasteful to me than having it cheekily sitting on the pillow.

Get a grip of yourself, I told myself sternly. Remember what you promised Paul. What will he think if you let a spider get the better of you? All you have to do is pick it up and throw it outside. It's only a spider after all. If only it wasn't so big, an inner voice protested, but I pretended not to hear.

I took a deep breath and tried to imagine I was a world famous biologist about to capture a prize that would make me rich and famous. It didn't help. The spider waved its other front leg at me in a contemptuous manner. It seemed to know that it was winning. I thought of my cousin. Right now hysteria didn't seem like such a bad option.

"Right Hannah," I said, still trying to sound brave. "When I say so, I want you to run downstairs and open the back door for me."

"Why?"

"So we can put the spider outside, of course."

"Won't he be cold?"

"No," I said firmly. "Spiders like it outside."

I moved toward the bed, trying to look determined. We eyed each other suspiciously, spider versus human. Right, I thought, here goes for the human race. Too frightened to breathe, I cupped my hands around the creature and scooped him off the bed. For one awful moment I thought I was going to faint but then I felt Hannah push past me, heading for the stairs.

The journey to the back door seemed to take a lifetime. Hannah took an age carefully dealing with the stairs one at a time whilst I was longing to race down three at once. Then it was through the hall, running through the lounge and finally into the kitchen. All the while I was aware of the spider, imprisoned between my sweaty palms. A new fear gripped me. What would I do if I crushed it? A vision too horrible to contemplate came to mind. I pushed the thought away and concentrated on Hannah. The kitchen door was locked and her small fingers were wrestling with the key.

"Hurry up, love." I tried to sound calm, a difficult feat when you can't hear your own voice above the sound of your heart beating.

At last there was a click and the door flew open. With a sigh of relief I threw the spider out into the garden.

For a long time Hannah and I stood and watched it: a poor, forlorn black spot huddled on the grey concrete. It didn't move.

"Is he dead?" Hannah whispered.

I shook my head, wondering if this tiny creature could possibly be the monster I had faced in Hannah's bedroom.

"I don't think so, love. I expect he's just a bit surprised."

Hannah shivered and tugged her cardigan tightly around herself.

"I think he must be cold. Shall we bring him back in again?"

"No," I squeaked. Fortunately, the idea of being picked up again seemed to spur the spider into action. He uncurled his legs and then slowly, almost disdainfully, stalked away. As we watched he turned to face us and rudely waved his front legs in our direction, then he disappeared into a crack in the garden wall.

I closed the door, not feeling at all victorious. Hannah gazed up at me, her face serious.

"You're very brave, Mummy," she said. The Torvill and Dean look was back, and I allowed myself to bask in its warmth as Hannah continued, "When there was a spider in my room before, Daddy said it would just go away if we left it alone."

"Oh, did he now," I said, coolly.

"Yes," Hannah continued. "Daddy wouldn't pick it up. I don't think he likes spiders, do you?"

"No, I don't suppose he does," I said. "I shall have to ask him when he gets home. Now, why don't you carry on with your game while I finish washing-up?"

As life returned to normal, I smiled secretly to myself. I would have stored up more than a few words about setting example by the time Paul got home; that was for sure.

**When is it My Turn?**

"What are you doing?" asked Bethany, as she danced into the small bedroom at the back of the house. She settled herself on the bed, sitting cross-legged, fingers plucking at a loose thread on the bedspread.

"What do you think I'm doing?" Mary replied automatically. She always tried to answer her four-year-old's questions with one of her own, believing it encouraged Bethany to reason things out for herself.

Bethany wrinkled her face thoughtfully. "You're putting all Jamie's clothes in there." She pointed at the suitcase that Mary was packing neatly.

"That's right."

"Why?"

Mary sighed. 'Why' was Bethany's new word. One she seemed determined to overuse. "Because Jamie is going home this afternoon."

Bethany frowned as she considered this. "Isn't this Jamie's home?" she asked after some time.

"Oh, Bethany, I've explained this to you a dozen times." Mary's voice carried a hint of exasperation. "Jamie only came to live with us because his mummy was ill, remember? Now his mummy is better again he's going home. Now please, no more questions, okay? Why don't you go and play with your dolls for a bit?"

As Bethany bounced off the bed, Mary regretted being so short with her daughter. She picked up another of Jamie's shirts and folded it neatly before putting it in the suitcase with a sigh. She'd known that Jamie wouldn't be staying long, and of course she was thrilled he was going home to his own family. Nevertheless, there was always part of her that mourned a little when it was time to say goodbye to a child who, however briefly, had been part of the family. Ah well, she thought, once Jamie was safely returned to his family, she would take Bethany to the park and perhaps treat her to an ice cream on the way home. Just the two of them – that would be good for them both.

Downstairs six-year-old Jamie was building an aeroplane out of Lego. Bethany walked into the room and sat beside him. She watched him fitting the brightly coloured bricks together for a few minutes before speaking.

"You're going away today," she told him, seriously.

"I know," Jamie replied casually. He reached for another brick. "My mum's coming at three o'clock."

"Have you got two mummies then?" Bethany asked.

"Of course not." Jamie pointed towards the stairs, indicating Mary. "She's not a real mum," he said. "She's a foster mum. She just looks after children until they go and live with their proper mum and dad."

"Don't you want to live here then?" she asked.

Jamie shrugged. "It's all right. But I'd rather be with my own mum."

Bethany thought about this for a moment. "Do I have a real mum somewhere?"

Jamie shrugged again. "Don't know."

"Well, I like it here," said Bethany firmly. She got up and went to the toy cupboard. Reaching in, she pulled out Charlotte, her favourite doll – the one with the dark hair and big brown eyes. Then she went and sat in the armchair with the saggy bottom and the cushions that smelled of dusty flowers. It was the chair her daddy always sat in to tell her a story before she went to bed. It was big and comfortable, and it made her feel safe.

"Don't worry, Charlotte," she whispered into the doll's ear. "We aren't going anywhere." But she frowned as she said it and tried to ignore the unpleasant feeling in her tummy; the same feeling that she had when she once got lost in Woolworths.

Jamie's mum arrived fifteen minutes early. Bethany knew this because Jamie had spent the last ten minutes staring at the clock and showing off because he could tell the time and she couldn't. At the sound of the doorbell, Bethany dropped the toy car she was playing with, snatched up Charlotte and climbed back onto the chair.

"I'm sorry I'm so early," Jamie's mum said as Mary opened the door. "I just couldn't wait any longer. I can't believe we're going to be together again."

Jamie was already on his feet. He ran to his mum as she came into the lounge, laughing loudly and wrapping himself around her legs as she tried to scoop him into a hug. Bethany watched solemnly from her chair. She didn't want Jamie to go away with this strange woman. She looked at Jamie's mum critically and decided that she was much too thin. Perhaps she didn't eat enough. If Jamie went to live with her, he might never get cakes at tea time.

"Say goodbye to Jamie," Mary said a few minutes later, beckoning Bethany over. His suitcase had already been taken out to the waiting car, and he was buttoned into his winter coat.

Reluctantly Bethany got out of the chair and walked over to Jamie. She looked up at the thin woman who was taking Jamie away. Suddenly frightened, she hid behind Mary.

"Come on, darling, don't be silly," Mary said, bending down to hug Jamie. "We'll all miss you," she said to him, planting a big kiss on his cheek. "You know you can always come and play, if you want to. I'm sure Bethany would like that."

Jamie nodded happily. "I'd like that too."

Bethany knew what was coming. She was going to have to say goodbye. Well, she wasn't going to do it. She didn't want Jamie to go, and maybe if she didn't actually say the words, then somehow it would be just like he'd gone to school. Before her mother could tell her to say goodbye, she slipped out of the room, and hurried upstairs.

"Bethany?"

79

She heard her mother call her name, but pretended she couldn't hear. When she reached the top of the stairs she hesitated. Her own room was to the left, but she didn't want to go in there right now. Instead she tiptoed into Jamie's room. It looked very tidy now that all his clothes and toys were gone. When she heard the front door open again, she climbed up on the bed and peered out of the window. Down below, she could see the two mums were standing on the pavement chatting; Jamie had climbed into the front seat of the bright red car that was parked in front of the house. He was pretending to drive, turning the steering wheel left and then right. When he pressed the horn, it made a mournful sound.

Bethany sighed and got off the bed. Suddenly she felt very sad and she didn't want to look at the car, or Jamie, or the woman was taking him away. She hurried out of Jamie's room and ran into her own, shutting the door firmly behind her.

The house seemed very quiet when Mary finally closed the front door. She sighed. Jamie might have only been with them for a few weeks but she would miss his bright chatter and the bang-crash tumble of having a boy around the house. Still it was very good that he was back with his own parents again. Her job was done, and the prognosis for his mother was looking very good.

Now, where was Bethany?

Her daughter was sure to miss Jamie too. The two children had got on really well. Perhaps the trip to the park would take her mind off things. After all, four-year-olds have very short memories, and besides, Bethany was used to children coming and going.

Mary checked the lounge but it was empty. Going upstairs, she pushed open the door to Bethany's room. Her daughter was busily pushing all her clothes into the suitcase which normally lived on top of the wardrobe. Mary studied the furniture as she went into the room, wondering how on earth Bethany had managed to get the case down. She shook her head and decided perhaps it was better not to worry about Bethany's climbing skills right now. She settled herself on the bed and watched as her daughter scrunched a freshly ironed blouse into a corner of the case.

"What are you doing?" she asked, realising it was the same question Bethany had asked her a few hours earlier.

"Packing my clothes," Bethany replied, without looking up.

Mary picked Charlotte up and idly began to smooth the doll's hair, but Bethany snatched the toy from her.

"I'm packing Charlotte too," she said.

Oh dear, something was obviously very wrong. Mary tried to put her arm round Bethany, but the little girl pulled away.

"I thought we might go to the park," Mary said, trying to sound cheerful.

"Don't want to." Bethany shoved Charlotte into the suitcase and closed the lid. As she tugged at the stiff, metal fasteners, her small face began to redden with the onset of tears. Suddenly she turned to Mary.

"When is it my turn?" she demanded.

"When is it your turn for what?" Mary asked, bemused by the question.

"My turn to go," Bethany said bitterly. Now the tears started to flow. "Jamie said you weren't a real mum. Now he's gone, it must be my turn next."

"Oh Bethany," Mary said, gathering her sobbing child up in her arms. This time there was no resistance. "Of course I'm your real mum."

Bethany hiccupped as she gulped air through her tears. "But all the children who come here leave again."

Bethany's words were like a blow to the stomach. Shaken, Mary hugged her tighter, wrestling with her own mixed emotions. How could she have been so stupid as to not realise the effect her work as a foster mother was

81

having on Bethany? It was true that she had looked after several children over the past few months, but it had never occurred to her that Bethany might think she did not belong to her. She lifted Bethany's tear-streaked face so that the little girl could see how serious she was.

"You are my very own precious little girl," she said firmly. "And you don't ever have to go away."

"I don't want to go away," Bethany sobbed.

"Then you won't," Mary said. "Other children come here because their own mummies and daddies can't look after them for some reason: like Jamie's mum getting sick. But when things are sorted out at their homes, they go back."

"But what if you get sick?"

"Well, Daddy would look after you. And I expect Auntie Louise would come and help him. Jamie came to stay with us because he didn't have any aunties and his daddy works on a boat so he couldn't be at home all the time."

Mary hugged Bethany again. "If you never remember anything else, I want you to remember that you're my daughter and I love you very much." She smiled as Bethany's arms tightened around her. "Now, dry your tears and we'll put all these clothes back into the cupboard, okay?"

"Okay," Bethany said, giving a small but relieved smile.

That night, Bethany sat on her daddy's lap in the big armchair and listened while he read her favourite story. Then she went happily upstairs to bed and snuggled down in the soft sheets with Charlotte beside her. Mary tiptoed into the room and kissed her on the cheek. Just as she was leaving the room, Bethany called softly to her.

"Mummy?"

"Yes, dear?"

"I'm glad you're my real mummy." In the amber light stealing through the curtains from the street lamp outside

82

her bedroom, Bethany could see the smile that lit up her mother's face.

"And I'm glad you're my real daughter," Mary said. "Sleep well my darling."

When the door had shut, Bethany put her arms round Charlotte. "You see," she whispered, her tummy no longer feeling as though there were a dozen butterflies inside it. "I told you we weren't going anywhere."

*Author's note about this story: When I was little, my parents were employed by Social Services as foster parents and they frequently took in children who needed care in emergency situations. Although I don't remember it, I was the little girl who asked her mother 'when is it my turn to leave?' I'm glad to say, I too discovered I didn't ever have to leave. When I was five years old, K. arrived. Short-term became long-term until one day she too discovered that she didn't have to leave. While sometimes it was hard to share my parents with other children, their legacy of caring has gifted me with a younger sister, and for that I am forever grateful.*

## Afraid

As Sara reached the top step she sighed with relief. For the first time since she had returned to her home town she felt she had made the right decision. Life in London had moved too quickly for her to be able to look at it without bias. Her home town was sleepy and quiet; here she could seek her answers.

She was standing on a concrete wall; it was about six feet high and several feet thick. Behind her the houses of the town were huddled together like children sharing a secret. In front of her stretched the sea, the wave-washed beach, and time to be alone. Stepping to the edge of the wall she took a deep breath, relaxed her muscles and then jumped. She landed heavily in the rain-soaked sand, and stumbled inelegantly forward, falling to her knees. She smiled wryly, remembering how blithely she used to make that jump as a child.

Climbing to her feet she brushed the sticky sand grains from her hands, and then turned to the north and began to walk. She knew the beach well. In minutes she would leave the golden stretch of sand, with its blue flag for cleanliness, and start walking through grass-bound dunes and ribbons of smooth, rounded pebbles. Again her instinct told her she was right to have come. The sun glistened cheerfully on the waves, the air was fresh and fragrant with salt, and she could feel herself attuning to her surroundings. At last she could organise her thoughts without distractions – or, more importantly, without Simon.

She walked on, savouring the taste and smell of the sea, and letting herself simply enjoy the wild, empty space. Closing her eyes, she tilted her head up to the sky and breathed deep. Oh to be a child again, young and worry-free.

"Hi!" A voice close to her left side broke sharply into her fragile solitude. Startled Sara opened her eyes. A young

85

man had cheekily fallen into step beside her. He was tall and slender, with perfect olive skin, shoulder length dark hair and just a hint of a beard. She halted, and was somewhat alarmed when he did too.

"Where did you come from?" she demanded, glancing back the way she'd just come. Had he been following her? Surely she would've noticed.

"Forgive me," he said. "I didn't mean to startle you." He smiled cheerfully, his dark hair blowing in the breeze as though it had a life of its own. "I saw you from above. You looked lost, so I thought I'd come and offer my assistance." He made an airy gesture that took in most of the surroundings.

Above? Sara squinted at the sandy cliffs some distance away. There was no obvious footpath down to the beach, but what else could he mean? "You must have good eyesight," she said, "but I'm not lost. Thank you for your concern." She turned to go, annoyed by the intrusion.

"May I walk with you?" he called, as she began to stride away. "Please?"

Common sense told her to say no. She'd wanted to be alone, and it was far from sensible to start wandering along a deserted beach with a total stranger. There had been a gentleness, a vulnerability, about the way he'd asked, though, and she surprised herself by nodding. "If you want." She walked quickly on.

Her new companion fell in step soundlessly at her side. "Why are you walking here?" he asked.

She shrugged. "It's a beach. It's a nice day. I – "

He cut her off with a wave of his hand. "Why are you *really* walking here?" he asked, his quick glance at her penetrating through her fake casualness.

She hesitated as her emotions swung through a kaleidoscope of options. How could she possibly answer given that the true response would be so complex? She was confused, afraid and, if she was honest with herself, he was right in saying that she was lost. Not physically,

86

though. The loss was of herself: Sara Kingston, twenty-four years old, about to be married.

"I…" she paused, trying but failing to find a word that reflected the depth of her emotion. "I just need to walk – sometimes."

The answer was just as trite as her previous attempt, and she felt as though she had blatantly lied to him. There was something about him that demanded a revelation of her inner self. A frown flickered across his face and then was gone. Silence hung like a thick blanket as they moved on. Sara's thoughts reeled incoherently within her. Questions rang unanswered like dark echoes in her brain and the lack of conversation weighed down on her shoulders. Finally she could bear it no longer. She stopped abruptly, turned and glared at him.

He stood motionless, returning her gaze. Swiftly she judged his appearance. He was slightly older than she was, athletic and attractive, but there was something else about him. There was an intangible strain, lightly veiled in his eyes, that spoke of suffering, of a shared pain.

"Who are you?" she demanded.

"I am whoever you desire me to be," he replied cryptically. Abruptly, he cartwheeled across the sand, landing lightly on his feet. "I can be the sun, lightness and life. Or I can be the night, silent, patient." His mood switched. Seriousness flooded across his face, etching it with lines of concern. "You must decide who you will choose. I am many things."

Sara shook her head, both annoyed and bemused. This was completely ridiculous. She had returned to the sea to find answers and here was a strange man presenting her with new questions. She decided to ignore his display and voiced a different question hoping to catch hold of reality as it passed by.

"Where do you live? In town? Or are you a visitor too?"

His mood remained serious as he replied. "I live where the door is open to me. Here and everywhere."

"So what's that? Some kind of riddle?" She stared at him, wondering if he wasn't perhaps insane.

Suddenly he reached forward and took her left hand. Holding it up to the sunlight he frowned at the engagement ring on her finger. "The ring has no life," he said, accusingly.

Sara snatched her hand away as though his touch was fire. How could he have seen the flaw in the ring? The diamond that had once glistened with an icy fire had turned dull and milky. When she'd first noticed, she'd tried to convince herself she was imagining things. Diamonds didn't cloud. Deep down, though, she'd known it was a sign – that the lack of clarity was coming from herself, from her own confusion about her relationship. She turned from him, determined to leave, but his hand touched her shoulder, holding her back.

"Why are you walking here?" he asked again.

Suddenly weary, Sara sank to the sand. He gazed down at her and it was as though his eyes would burn her flesh with their intensity. She wrapped her arms around herself, hugging her knees to her chest. The ring on her finger was protected by the crook of her arm, safely hidden from his sight. "I'm here because as a young girl I used to come to the beach to find peace. When I was confused and angry I walked here and the sea washed away my pain. I need to feel washed now."

She looked up at him, expecting him to speak, but he remained silent, so she continued. "I am going to be married soon. I love Simon, my fiancé, so much that sometimes I think I couldn't bear to live without him and yet – I'm so afraid." She turned her face towards the sea. "Fear chokes my love when he smiles at me. When he holds me I feel as though it will strangle me. I don't know myself anymore. How can love endure? Isn't it too fragile to stand the trial of a lifetime of marriage?"

She turned back, meeting his gaze, wondering why she was sharing so much with him, and yet suddenly finding it completely natural to do so. He crouched beside her, and drew her left hand from its hiding place. He held it gently cradled in his own, the diamond against his palm.

"Your fear is a cancer," he said quietly. "If you let it grow, it will destroy you. You must throw it into the waves as you did with your childhood pain. Let it go! As for your love, a gift of this kind is precious. Real love will endure more than the human mind can comprehend. Love is purified in suffering."

He released his hold on her and slowly lifted his left hand before her. She gasped involuntarily at the sight, wondering how she had failed to see such a wound. Both the palm and the back of his hand were marred by ugly, white scar tissue. It was as if his entire hand had been penetrated by something sharp and deadly. She reached tentatively for his other hand; that too was marked by cruelty.

She felt tears burn hotly on her face as she saw within his eyes qualities that she had never before encountered. She longed to speak, to cry out in protest at the pain he had suffered but she had no voice.

"Never be afraid of love," he said, "because love is the key to life. Because of love I accepted the pain which gave me these scars. You must be brave. If you love Simon you will risk the pain and the scars."

"I don't have the strength," Sara protested.

"Love is your strength. It gives you what you need when you need it. Love is the only foundation you need for your life. Hold it tight, Sara, and drive away the fear."

Suddenly he climbed to his feet, and holding out his hand drew her up. "Will you run with me?" he asked, searching her face with concern.

"Run?" She gave a bark of laughter, but then, fighting down the tears she nodded.

"Come then." He broke into a jog, gesturing for her to follow.

Feeling foolish, she matched her pace to his: pebbles crunched beneath her shoes, a lone seagull wheeled overhead, the breeze caught at her hair and she tasted salt on her tongue. She ran and ran, relishing the burn of her muscles, until with a laugh of joy she suddenly felt herself released. His words were strange and confusing but slowly she was beginning to understand the meaning hidden in them. She was free to trust, free to build a marriage, free of a childhood in a broken home, free of the pain of parents who had fought over her and for her.

At first she felt she could have run forever, but gradually exuberance drifted away and she began to lag behind. Then exhaustion hit her like a wave and she slowed to a stop. The young man glanced behind him and smiled, but he did not slow his pace.

"Wait," she cried, desperately trying to catch her breath. "The wedding – will you come?"

His smile grew wider as he called back to her. "If the door is open I can pass through."

And then he was gone. Sara was alone on the beach, squinting into the sun. She raised her left hand, and smiled. The diamond in her ring sparkled brightly, its centre clear and beautiful.

## The Homecoming

A shaft of autumn sunlight crept through the gap in the curtains, chasing the shadows from the room. On the bed a figure turned and groaned inwardly. Was it morning already? Suddenly a pair of brown eyes snapped open as conscious thought slipped through the blankets of sleep. It was Saturday. John was coming home today.

Phillippa sat up quickly and reached for the clock. It was seven-thirty. His plane was due at noon, and there were still so many things to do. She hugged her knees to her chest with a thrill of excitement. *John was coming home – at last*!

Slipping into her dressing gown, she headed for the bathroom, humming happily to herself. As she crossed the landing, a bedroom door opened and a head appeared in the gap.

"Morning, dear. You sound cheerful." It was Mrs Lawson, John's mother.

"I feel cheerful," she said with a smile. She nodded towards the door further up the landing. "Is it all right if I have a bath?"

"Of course it is, love. You don't need to ask. You're nearly family to us now."

A few minutes later, Philippa sank into a bath full of hot, fragrant water, a thoughtful expression on her face. Nearly family: was that really the way the Lawsons looked upon her? She knew Mrs Lawson was aware that John had not contacted her since he had left home. So how could she consider her to be nearly family?

"There's no point in me writing letters," John had said on their last evening together for six months. "The village is fifty miles from the nearest town and, even from there, the post is taken only once a month. Then it will be weeks before it reaches you. It goes overland to the coast. The chances of it actually making it home are virtually nil."

91

"It doesn't matter," she had replied. "Just think of me every day."

"I'll do better than that. I'll think about you every minute!"

So she had agreed not to expect a letter, but as the months passed and John's photograph began to fade in the sunlight that fell on her desk, she couldn't help but wish for just one short note.

The memory of that evening vanished as Phillippa brought herself back to the present. In a few more hours he would be back. Six months had passed – would he still care about her?

"It's a great chance, Pip," he'd said. "I'll be able to see what real medicine is all about. Africa is such an incredible place and I'll be of use out in the desert villages even with only three years of medical school behind me."

"Yes, love, I can see that. I just wish you didn't have to go so far. Or for so long."

"It's only six months, Pip. It'll fly by, you'll see."

But it hadn't flown by. Sometimes Phillippa thought that each day was a week and each week a year. Would he have changed? Of course he would have, she told herself. Anybody living in the African wilderness would be changed by the experience.

"Breakfast is ready, Phillippa!" Mrs Lawson called up the stairs.

"Coming!" she called.

Dressed in a red skirt and a black t-shirt that she knew John had always liked her wearing, Phillippa joined the Lawsons for breakfast.

"Excited love?" Mrs Lawson asked. Phillippa nodded. "It will be good to have him home again," Mrs Lawson continued, "even though it will be for such a short time. The new term starts so soon. He'll be back to medical school before we know it."

Yes, Philippa thought sadly. Here one week, gone the next. Oh John, please be the same person that went out to Africa.

Breakfast dragged on. Everybody had something that they wanted to fit into their week with John. His brother, Andy, had managed to obtain two tickets for the big football match the following weekend. Mr Lawson wanted John's advice on buying a car and planned to take him for a day's fishing. Even Mrs Lawson intended to claim his company for a day at the local trade fair. Phillippa sat silently, listening to their enthusiastic chatter. The early morning excitement had vanished and now she was only fearful of meeting him again.

"Phillippa? Phillippa? Are you all right, dear?"

Suddenly she realised that she was the focus of attention. She reddened with embarrassment. "Sorry, I was miles away."

"You've hardly touched your breakfast," Mrs Lawson chided gently.

"I'm fine, really. I'm just excited that's all," she lied.

The airport terminal seemed unusually full for an autumn afternoon. A few enquiries led them to the gate from which John would emerge. The family gathered together in a tight knot, radiating their impatience. Phillippa stood to one side, her mood alienating her from their bright conversation. How could they understand how she felt? They would always be his parents and his brothers, whereas she was just his girlfriend – a relationship that could be ended with a few brief words.

"It will be all right, Phillippa." Mrs Lawson's voice startled her from the darkness of her thoughts. The older woman studied her intently for a moment, and then smiled sympathetically. "I can see it in your face. You're worried that his feelings for you will have changed, aren't you? John will be different, but it doesn't necessarily have to be a bad change. You'll see, Phillippa. He'll still love you."

"I hope so," she said, appreciating the reassurance.

"Here they come," Andy called, excitedly. "I can't see John, though. Where is he?"

People began to emerge from the exit in ones and twos, their faces weary from travel, but smiles breaking out as they spotted friends and relatives waiting for them. The noise in the lounge increased as greetings were called out and chatter exploded. It seemed to Phillippa that everyone around her was caught up in rapturous welcomes except for the Lawsons. And then she saw him.

His face was leaner than she remembered. Brown, weathered skin and bleached blond hair spoke of long hours under the desert sun. He looked older, less boyish.

"John!" Andy slipped beneath the barrier and flung his arm about his brother's shoulders. "Welcome home! We've all missed you!"

The sense of not belonging increased as Andy dragged John over to the family group. Self-conscious Phillippa stood to one side as the Lawsons gathered round. It seemed a life-time that she stood politely smiling until, at last, John saw her standing there.

He smiled almost shyly as he broke free from his family.

"Hello, Phillippa. I'm glad you're here."

Phillippa, she thought, anguished. John had never called her that. She had always been Pip to him.

She flushed, feeling as though he was a stranger. "I hope you don't mind me coming. It was your mum's idea."

"Mind? Of course not. It's great to see you."

Then the bustle descended again. Suitcases were grabbed by eager hands and John was guided away to the car. Phillippa followed, a forced smile on her face. He's just exhausted, she told herself. He must have been working incredibly hard. That was why he hadn't hugged her or kissed her. Her heart was heavy, though – he seemed so cold, so polite. *Oh John, have we lost everything so soon?*

The evening passed quickly. John's favourite meal was served for dinner and throughout it he was barraged with questions, news and plans.

As the plates were cleared away, he rose from the table.

"It's great to be home," he said, "but if you don't mind, I really need to go to bed. I can't remember the last time I slept."

He turned to go, resting his hand lightly on Phillippa's shoulders as he passed. His fingers squeezed gently. "I'll see you tomorrow, Phillippa?"

She nodded. Was he asking because he wanted her to be here or was he secretly hoping she'd be gone? "Yes, I'll be here," she said, then looked away, fearful his face would confirm her worst fear.

That night, sleep eluded her as worried thoughts chased through her mind. Six months, she thought bitterly, and now they were like strangers. She was afraid to think about what might happen in the morning, afraid to meet this distant person again, the man who called her Phillippa. He was tired, that was all, she told herself severely, yet surely he could have held her for a moment and told her he still cared. She sighed heavily.

"I loved you, John," she whispered into the darkness. "I wish I knew where you've gone."

It was early when she rose. She pulled back the curtains to reveal a cold, grey morning, heavy clouds hung oppressively over the neighbourhood. Rain splashed mournfully against the glass, distorting her view of the garden. She dressed, pulling on the first clothes that came to hand – a pair of old jeans and the same t-shirt from the day before – and then she tiptoed onto the landing. The sounds of the sleeping family stirred the otherwise silent house, and despite herself she smiled at the rumble of Mr Lawson's snores. Quietly, she made her way down the stairs and through to the kitchen. The door was slightly ajar – presumably Mrs Lawson was up and about. She tended to be the early bird.

Casually Phillippa strolled into the kitchen, the fragrant smell of coffee meeting her nose. She stopped abruptly. John was sitting at the kitchen table. He glanced up, the surprise on his face mixing with an expression that looked suspiciously like guilt. In front of him was a tangle of string and piles of brightly coloured paper. Quickly he pushed everything into a heap and stood.

"You're up early, Pip," he said.

"I could say the same thing about you," she said, smiling shyly. *He'd called her Pip!* She gestured towards the table. "What are you doing?"

"Oh, nothing." He moved around the table, blocking her view of the intriguing mass of paper.

She raised an eyebrow at that. Crossing the kitchen, she poured herself a mug of coffee and then moved to sit at the table. John circled in front it, trying to keep his secret hidden from her. She laughed at the absurdness of it all.

"John, it's seven o'clock in the morning. I haven't seen you for six months. Are we really going to engage in a dance around the kitchen table?"

He reddened and stepped aside. "Sorry, it's just – Please, sit down." He pulled a chair out for her. "Thing is, the reason I'm up so early is because of you, but I seem to be making rather a mess of things." He sank onto another chair. "I was so tired last night – you must've thought I was a real pig. I don't think we said more than a dozen words to each other."

"It was all a bit strange," she admitted. "Your family were so pleased to see you, and I didn't want to get in the way, and yet – "

"You'd never get in the way," he said softly. He smiled warmly, but then gestured at the table. "I actually got up early to wrap something up for you, but as you're here, well, perhaps it's better to just give it to you without giftwrap." He pushed the brightly coloured paper to one side, uncovering a tatty, brown notebook. "It doesn't look much, does it?" He held the book out to her.

She took it from him. Its spine was missing, and she was worried it might fall apart in her hands. She opened the battered cover carefully. Writing covered the inside pages, and she recognised the handwriting immediately. "Your diary?" she asked.

"Not exactly," he said.

She started to read: *Dear Pip, I've only been here a day and already I'm missing you so much. I don't know how I'll get through the next few months. I guess that when you are away from someone who means so much to you...*

She turned the page, and then the next. Each one was dated carefully and opened with the words: Dear Pip. She looked up at John. He was watching her, a grin of embarrassment on his face.

"I know I said that I wouldn't write, but that I'd think of you every day, actually every minute of every day. Well, once I was out there, I realised how selfish I was being. How were you to know that I did think of you every day? The problem was getting letters to you really was difficult. It was miles to the nearest town, and most times the post office, such as it was, wouldn't be open. But I wanted you to share in everything so I wrote these letters to you instead, every night before I went to bed. It kept me sane at times, Pip – knowing that you were here, hoping that we'd be together again."

She didn't know what to say, but the fear that had gripped her the previous day lifted. He did care. Six months apart had been hard in so many ways, but now he was back, and not only that, she had precious evidence in her hands that he hadn't once forgotten her.

"I wrote the last page on the plane," he said.

She turned the pages of the book, intending to look, but he reached out and stopped her.

"No, don't look. I want to say the words to you in person." He took her hand, and then stood, drawing her to her feet. "I love you, Pip, and I don't want to spend another six months, six weeks or even six hours without you. Will you marry me?"

She looked into his eyes, studying the changes she could see there. He was older and more mature, and she did not doubt that his time away had changed him. Perhaps it had changed her too. Underneath it all, though, they were still the same two people who had fallen in love. She stepped into his waiting arms.

"I've missed you too, John. Of course I'll marry you."

*Author's note: It seems strange in these days of email and mobile phones to look back at a story written before those times. Being out of touch with a loved one for a long period of time is thankfully something few of us have to experience. The inspiration behind this tale came from knowing that a doctor friend of mine was planning to go to Africa to work with a volunteer organisation. He was terrible at writing letters and so I knew I'd hear precious little from him while he was overseas.*

## The Waiting Game

Barry stood alone on the cold station platform. A northerly wind gusted along the train tracks, tumbling a discarded paper cup in its wake. His feet and hands had grown stiff and painful in the bitter wind, but still he waited. He felt he had been there all his life: standing cold and isolated, waiting for this moment to arrive.

He shifted his weight onto his right foot, stamping the left one to warm it. A long way in the distance he could see workmen in bright orange coats. He wondered idly what they were doing so close to the track when a train was due, and he tried not to be bothered by their intrusion. Soon the train would come and then it would all be over. Today the waiting would end.

He was nineteen again, talking with his best mate over yet another lukewarm cup of coffee. Gavin was home from university for the Christmas holidays and full of stories of his new life – and his new girlfriend.

"You don't understand," Gavin said again. "Jenny is special."

"You said Cara was special," Barry protested, unwilling to believe that Gavin had started seeing another girl.

Gavin stared down at his coffee and shrugged. "She was. I mean she still is. It's just that…" He trailed off.

"Just that once you met Jenny you didn't want to see her any more, right?" Barry said for him. "So how did Cara take that?"

Gavin had the grace to look miserable. Picking up a teaspoon, he put a sixth spoonful of sugar into his coffee and stirred it absentmindedly.

"Please tell me you've told her," Barry said, barely able to hide his dismay at Gavin's two-timing.

Gavin shook his head. "I wouldn't know what to say." He looked up, his face pathetically appealing. "I thought perhaps you might tell her."

"Me! No way. I'm not doing your dirty work."

"Look, Barry, I'll be blunt. You like Cara, don't you? If you asked her out it might help. You know, make her feel wanted."

Barry studied Gavin's face, wondering if his friend realised how cruel his words were. He had been in love with Cara from the moment he first saw her by Gavin's side. But she was so obviously besotted with his friend he'd kept his feelings hidden. So well hidden that even Gavin hadn't guessed the truth. And now Gavin was trying to pass Cara on to him like a second-hand car.

"Well?" Gavin asked.

"I'll do what I can to help," Barry said. "But you must break things off with her."

The first time he called Cara, he wasn't sure that she would want to even speak to him. He was, after all, the best friend of her ex-boyfriend. Truth was, though, she'd let most of her other friendships slide while she was going out with Gavin, and she seemed pleased to hear a friendly voice, and glad of his company. She cried a lot in those first few days after the break-up. Barry sat and listened as she tried to work out why Gavin no longer wanted her, and what it was about Jenny that was so much better. He bought her ice cream, sat through chick flicks with her, and kept his feelings to himself.

"I was such a fool," she confided to him one day. "I'd even started looking in estate agents' windows, thinking maybe Gavin and I would ..." She laughed bitterly, shaking her head at her own words. "Well, I won't make that mistake again." She took Barry's hand and squeezed it affectionately. "I'm glad we're just friends. Life is so much easier when love isn't involved."

Barry nodded, and carried on pretending friendship was all he wanted in return, while deep inside he ached to tell her the truth. Every time he tried to summon up enough courage, though, something would hold him back. Perhaps it was fear of destroying the understanding they had or perhaps it was the hopeful way that Cara sometimes asked after Gavin, unwittingly reminding him that he was her only contact with Gavin.

There was a train. Barry hugged his arms about himself, feeling his stomach lurch with tense nerves. He watched it stop in the distance, some invisible signal preventing it from finishing its journey.

Was it the one? A tremble ran through him. Yes, this one would end all the waiting.

"I've decided what I'm going to do," Cara had said some weeks after the break up. She'd bent down to pick up a pebble from the beach and then she flung it wildly out to sea. Barry watched it fly, taking in the careless way she threw it away. She turned towards him, her face reddened by the chill wind. "I'm going to Leeds – to train as a nurse."

He was shocked by the suddenness of her decision. The chill wind suddenly bit into him, making him shiver. He wrapped his arms around his chest. She was going away, leaving him.

"Leeds?" he managed to say. Anger suddenly flared, hot against the ice in his bones. "And how much does the fact that Gavin lives there affect your choice?"

She turned away from him, but he grabbed her by the shoulders and pulled her back to face him.

"He's got someone else, Cara. Can't you understand that?"

"No," she cried. "No, I can't. That's why I have to go. I have to see for myself that he loves someone else." She

101

burst into tears. "Please understand, Barry. This is the only way I'll ever get Gavin out of my life."

No, he would never understand, but he was unable to give her a reason to stay. He looked at her, seeing the determination in her mascara-smudged expression. Gavin was as much between them now as he had been the first time they met.

The train was moving again. It was coming slowly into the station. He remembered his letter, written rashly one evening after Cara had phoned to chat. Her training was nearly finished, she said, and then she casually mentioned that she might go abroad for a year or two. After she'd rung off he suddenly realised he had to tell her the truth. He was going to lose her whatever he did, so in one crazy tumble he put all his feelings down in black and white and rushed to the postbox before he could change his mind.

He finished the letter with a plea. If she could ever feel the same way about him as he did about her she was to meet him. He'd named a date in November, and then spent hours worrying. What if she couldn't get away that day? But it was too late. The letter had gone.

The train was nearly in now. Its brakes squealing and carriages shuddering as it came to a halt. He could barely breathe. It was so nearly finished and he was ready. One by one, people climbed from the train, some pulling heavy cases behind them, some with friends or family. Some were alone, just like him.

Cara wasn't amongst the passengers heading for the exits. His heart sank. He knew he'd been a fool. Cara loved Gavin. She always had and she always would. He knew they'd met up in Leeds. He knew too that Jenny had been replaced by Laura and then by Kate, but that Cara was patiently waiting, patiently hoping that one day Gavin would look at her again. Well, perhaps it was better that she wasn't here. Maybe she couldn't move on with her life, but he could get on with his. The waiting was over for him.

He turned and slowly began to walk up the platform towards the far exit, following the guard who was shutting the open carriage doors of the empty train. Suddenly, though, a door was flung open again, nearly hitting him as he passed. He stood motionless, his brain refusing to accept what his eyes were seeing. Cara!

"Hi," she said, strangely shy. "I nearly missed the stop. I was so nervous about getting here that I knocked my bag over and everything fell out." She patted the large straw bag at her side, and then pushed a suitcase towards him. "Could you take this?"

He nodded, and still unable to think of anything to say, lifted the case onto the platform. Cara stepped off the train, and then together they began to walk towards the exit.

"I got your letter," she said, sounding rather embarrassed. "Did you really mean all those things you said?"

"Every word," Barry replied, his heart pounding.

Cara smiled as she looked at him. "The train was late. I thought you might have gone," she said. "You'll never know how worried I was that you might've thought I wasn't coming and decided not to wait." Shyly she slipped her hand into his and squeezed it gently. "Have you been waiting long?"

"No," he said. "Not long at all."

## Throw-away Romance

There was a bouquet of beautiful fresh flowers in my wheelie bin. Not just any old bouquet either, but one of those posh ones from the florist in the high street. Who on earth would throw such a thing away? And why would they put them in *my* bin?

Puzzled, I studied my neighbours' houses, hoping for some clue to the mystery. Mrs Armstrong in the adjoining semi often had flowers in a vase in her front window. Usually, though, they were cheap and cheerful chrysanthemums that her grandkids had picked up from a petrol station on their way to Sunday lunch. She certainly wouldn't have thrown out such a fabulous bunch of blooms. Steve, my other neighbour, had saved like crazy to take three years off work to study for a degree; he was hardly a candidate for floral fly-tipping either.

Oh well, whoever they belonged to, they clearly weren't wanted. I retrieved them from their dank surroundings, flicking a stray baked bean off the strawberry coloured ribbon tied around their stems. Closing the lid on the pong of rotting potato peelings and musty teabags, I breathed in their scent – the Turkish Delight aroma of the creamy white roses mingled with the summery scent of lilac freesias. They were absolutely gorgeous, and I had the perfect vase for them. For once Mrs Armstrong wouldn't be the only person with flowers on display. Hooray for a bit of unexpected recycling.

Three hours later my doorbell rang. It was Steve. "Run out of milk again?" I joked, always happy to see him. We'd become pretty good friends over recent months. Sometimes he'd drop in for five minutes and end up staying five hours. We'd start talking and that would be it – the day would rush by before we realised it.

"Not today," he said, my usual teasing welcome failing to raise a smile.

"What's up?" I asked with concern.

"This is really awkward," he said. He glanced furtively at his house. "Can I come in?"

"Of course you can. I'll make some tea." I headed down the hallway towards the kitchen, expecting him to follow.

"I can't stay," he called.

I turned and was surprised to see he was still standing just inside the front door. "What's wrong?" I asked, my mind conjuring up a dozen disaster scenarios. "What's going on?"

He folded his arms across his chest, hugging himself. "It's about the flowers," he said.

"The flowers?" I repeated, momentarily puzzled.

"The ones you found in your bin," he said.

I stared at him for a moment. "How did you know that's where they came from?"

He sighed heavily. "Jen threw them in there last night. We – umm – we'd had a bit of a row."

"Oh dear," I said, sympathetically. I'd become a bit of an agony aunt to Steve since the tempestuous Jen had stormed into his life. However, throwing an expensive bouquet of flowers into a wheelie bin was a bit over the top even by her hot-headed standards. "And I suppose now she's calmed down she's had second thoughts and wants them back."

He grimaced, which I took to mean that yes, that was exactly what she wanted. I shook my head in bemusement.

"You know, it would serve her right if I kept them," I said, heading into the lounge to fetch them. "She knows you haven't got money to throw around, right? Yet when you go to all the trouble and expense of giving her a beautiful bouquet, she thanks you by dumping them in the bin – and not even your bin, but mine." I grabbed the flowers from the vase, and turned. Steve was now standing in the doorway of the lounge. He looked completely and utterly miserable.

106

"Sorry, Kate, but I didn't come to get the flowers back."

"You didn't?" Now I felt a complete idiot. "Then why are you here?"

He stared down at the floor for a long moment, but then looked up. "Thing is, it wasn't an accident that she put them in *your* bin."

"Oh?" The flowers were beginning to drip water onto the floorboards. It occurred to me that I ought to do something about that, but I couldn't seem to move.

"She was making a point," he said.

"What sort of point?" I asked, although deep down I already knew. She'd obviously guessed the truth. The thing is I've fancied Steve for months now. Who wouldn't? He's nice looking, intelligent, funny. He's also determined to always see the best in people, which is fine until someone like Jen Dixon decides to use him as a door mat.

"She said that I should've given the flowers to you since I spend so much time round here."

"Surely she isn't jealous of me?" I said, trying to make it sound as though the idea was ridiculous. I'd tried so very hard to be good. Not once had I made a move on him. Not even that time when she'd been particularly spiteful and he so obviously wanted comfort. I'd valued his friendship too much to risk scaring him off suggesting that maybe, just maybe, I could offer him more than Jen.

"I guess so." He nodded miserably. "I tried to explain that we were just good friends, but you know how she can be sometimes." His face was sombre. "I'm sorry Kate, but I think it would be best if we perhaps didn't meet up for a while - just until this blows over."

My heart plummeted. Things like this didn't just 'blow over'. The game was up. Jen had recognised me as competition and wanted me out of his life, and since Jen always got her own way, well, this was it then. No more Steve popping round for a chat. No more Steve teaching me how to fix my car in exchange for lessons on the difference between weeds and flowers in his garden. No more jokes about running out of milk.

"I'm really sorry, Kate."

He reached out, obviously intending to give me a sympathetic hug. I raised a hand, fending him off. Somehow, I dredged up a smile. "It's okay. I understand, really I do." Oh yes, I understood only too well. The sweet fragrance of the flowers suddenly seemed sickly and cloying. "Here you go," I said, thrusting them at him.

He shook his head. "No, you should keep those."

"No," I corrected him forcefully. "I shouldn't."

He hesitated, but then took them. "I really am sorry," he said, turning to the door.

"Steve, just one thing," I blurted quickly, hurt vying with anger at the unfairness of it all.

"Yes?" he asked half-turning back

"If a woman throws your flowers in the bin to make a point, she really doesn't deserve to have them - or you."

"Kate…"

"What's more," I said before I could think better of it. "*I* would never throw your flowers in the bin. In fact, if you were to buy me flowers I'd treasure them, just like I treasure your friendship – just like I'd treasure you given half a chance." There, I'd said it.

He stared at me for a long moment. "Kate – I – " He sighed wearily, shaking his head before finally saying, "She's waiting for me."

"Then you'd better decide what it is you want." I threw the words into the air – a veiled challenge, an appeal for him to see things differently, to stand up for himself.

It's funny the things that make you realise you've fallen in love. With my ex-boyfriend, it was when I found myself listening to the country music that he adored and I hated. With Steve, it was hearing the sound of the front door closing as he left.

I sank onto my sofa and hugged a cushion to my chest, trying to muffle the sudden, unwelcome pain of his absence. I felt a complete and utter fool. Had I seriously thought a few minutes of honesty would be competition for Jen and all her charms? Right at that moment I wanted nothing more than to run away and never see Steve again.

When I eventually stopped crying, the logical part of my brain kicked in. Not seeing Steve was probably going to be impossible since we lived next door to each other. Moving house certainly wasn't an option – affordable houses this close to work were like hen's teeth. No, I'd just have to swallow my embarrassment and get on with life. I was hardly the first woman to suffer from unrequited love. I was mature. I could get over this. And if Jen didn't want Steve seeing me, that was fine, because right now I didn't want to see him.

Two whole weeks went by without me even catching a glimpse of him. I started going to work early so I wouldn't bump into him in the street in the mornings. The office was busy so I found a hundred and one reasons to work late too. In fact it really wasn't hard to fill up my days, and on the odd occasions when the doorbell rang and I thought I saw his shadow behind the glass in the door, I didn't answer it.

The following Saturday I cleaned my house until it was sparkling. Pleased with my hard work, I gathered up my rubbish and took it out to the wheelie bin. I was half way down the path when I spotted the red and gold helium balloon that had somehow got caught in the bin handles. Great, first someone else's flowers, now someone else's party balloon. I stalked down the rest of the path, grabbed the balloon's ribbon and gave it a yank to free it. It didn't come loose. That was odd. I tugged again, harder this time. Oh, it was tied to the bin. Someone had obviously put it here on purpose. Puzzled I paused to read the writing on its shiny metallic surface. 'I love you', it said.

Well, that made no sense at all. Annoyed at the mystery, I opened the bin to throw my rubbish into it, but instead of potato peelings and smelly bin bags, I found myself looking at a bunch of beautiful crimson peonies. They were protected from the rubbish beneath by a sturdy cardboard box. What on earth was going on? If this was some kind of joke —

I reached into the bin, retrieved the flowers and found a small white envelope tucked amongst the blooms. My name was on the envelope. My hands were shaking as I opened the envelope and pulled out the small square card from inside. On it was written:

> *'Dear Kate. It's over with Jen. You made me realise I was in danger of throwing away something of real value. I know you're avoiding me and I probably deserve it, but I'm hoping you can forgive me for not recognising that the girl for me was living right next door. Steve.'*

*Oh Steve.* I glanced up and saw he was standing in the doorway of his house, watching me uncertainly. I hesitated for a moment, not knowing what to do, but then, with trembling fingers, I untied the balloon. Carrying both the balloon and the flowers, I opened the small gate that led into his front garden, and then walked up the path towards him.

"They're beautiful," I said, when I reached him. "Are they from your garden?" I'd pointed the budding plants out to him a couple of weeks earlier.

He nodded. "You told me how much you love peonies, but I wasn't sure if I was doing the right thing. If you'd rather have a bunch from the florist - "

"These are much nicer," I said, truthfully.

He gestured towards the card in my hand. "So, what do you say? Is there a chance for me or have I blown it?"

"I think the balloon says it all," I said, offering it back to him.

For the briefest of moments, he looked puzzled, but then he suddenly realised what I meant. He grinned broadly, took the balloon and released it. Hand in hand we watched it soar into the sky.

## Seagulls and Celebrations

"I could stay home today," Mark offers. He's sitting at the breakfast table, dressed for work, but clearly reluctant to go. "There's a bit of a lull at work. No one would mind."

"No need," I say overly bright. He's trying so very hard to be thoughtful, and I love him for it. But why doesn't he understand I just want today to be like any other day? I don't want to remember, and I most certainly don't want him under my feet all day shooting me sympathetic looks.

"Well, if you're sure?" He sets his empty coffee cup on the kitchen table, brushes toast crumbs from the dark wool of his trouser leg, and then gets to his feet.

I scoop the car keys from their hook by the door, and hand them to him. "You're going to be late."

He sighs. "Kaz -" he begins, clearly planning to make yet another offer to remain.

"I'm fine." I flinch at the snappiness in my tone, but I'm equally determined that he should go. I manage a smile. "Sorry, it's just that I have a lot to do today."

"Okay." He kisses my cheek, then turns and ruffles Jamie's hair. "Be good for your mother."

Jamie shoots me a dark look. A school inset day is a holiday in his books, and I'm not playing ball by refusing his request for a day out at the local theme park. I feel guilty and wonder if I should try to explain how I feel, but he's only ten years old, and I don't want to burden him with my grief. Instead I use work as an excuse to hide away, telling him I have a lot to do, and asking him to amuse himself for the day. Is that selfish? Perhaps so, but I don't have the strength right now to face up to such questions.

From the hallway comes the sound of the front door banging shut. Mark has gone. Jamie shovels the last spoonful of cereal into his mouth, getting to his feet as he does so. His chair scrapes harshly against the floor tiles as he pushes away from the table. Wearing socks but no slippers, he skates across the ceramic tiles of the kitchen floor, heading for the lounge and his X-box. I'm left alone, facing the calendar and its list of birthdays for the month. Aunt Joan on the third, Mark's on the twelfth, and in the neat little square for today, my mother's name.

I swallow the grief, and tell myself it is just another day like any other. I can't fool myself, though. Memories are too sharp, too insistent. This time last year we met for lunch in her favourite café and then we spent the afternoon wandering through the Tate Modern. There was a special exhibition of Dali's artwork taking place, and we drifted leisurely through the display, savouring the surreal scenes and exclaiming over the brilliance of his imagination. In the gift shop at the end of our visit I purchased a souvenir calendar for her, another small birthday gift to add to the bouquet of roses that I'd given her earlier from all of us – Mark, Jamie and me.

The calendar now hangs on the wall next to my computer in the small bedroom that I use as a study. The pleasure I take from the exotic images is tempered by the knowledge that its original owner is not here to enjoy the final three months of elephants on stilts, melting watches and flying tigers.

With a sigh I head upstairs, checking in on Jamie on the way. His back is to me, his attention absorbed by Jedi knights and space battles. In his world you can die a hundred times over, returning to life at the press of a button. If only reality was the same.

As I pull out my desk chair, I glance out of the window. Our house is one of six that huddle together in a semi-circle at the end of a close. There are neatly mowed lawns and clipped shrubs between us and the neighbours opposite. I watch as Tom Bates hurries from number eight. He climbs into his dark green Mondeo and starts the engine. With a quick glance over his shoulder, he reverses out of the driveway, and then speeds off to work, just as he does every Friday morning. The world goes on, people doing every day routine things.

I push my memories away and join them, hoping that an hour or so of tedious numbers will help me bury the pain of her absence.

I'm wrestling with a spreadsheet when the gulls arrive in a noisy, squabbling mass of white and grey feathers. They swoop onto the roof of number eight, jostling for space on the ridge tiles. They call to each other, loud and raucous, not caring that they are interrupting my working day. Memories flash at the sound. I'm seven years old, waiting on one side of a raised bridge as a fishing boat chugs slowly into harbour, gulls following in its wake, cawing with greedy anticipation of its catch. I'm holding my mother's hand, impatient to be on the beach. She's smiling, happy to have escaped the washing and cleaning, the scrimping and saving, for a few brief hours.

I glare out of the window, the memories as bittersweet as sour cherries. There are at least fifteen gulls perched on the roof top now. Two stretch out their wings as though guarding territory. Another preens its breast feathers with a rapid urgency. A third turns awkwardly on the narrow ridge, loses its balance and takes flight. It loses height and then suddenly soars upwards. A nonchalant tilt of a wing brings it back to the roof and it lands again, eyeing the other birds with indignation as though daring them to suggest the impromptu flight wasn't planned.

They are herring gulls, judging from their size. That's odd. I've lived here for over ten years now, and rarely seen a gull of any sort, other than as an occasional smudge of white when the local farmers are ploughing the wheat fields out towards the villages. Mark's job bought us to this large inland town. We're bang smack in the middle of the country, as far from the sea as it is possible to be. There's

115

no scent of salt in the air here, no tang of ozone – just petrol fumes and people, and the ever-present sound of the motorway. So what on earth is a flock on herring gulls doing on my neighbour's rooftop?

A single bird releases a plaintive cry into the crisp autumn air. As one the birds take to the sky, wheeling and spinning against the steel grey clouds.

'Aren't they beautiful', says my mother's voice in my head.

'Pesky creatures', I reply silently, remembering how the local council used to rant about the expense of cleaning their droppings off buildings and street furniture. I hear her gentle laughter in response.

'You never did understand.'

'Understand what?' I ask, but there's no reply.

I close my eyes. No, I don't understand. A few brief months ago, she was alive and well. Then she got sick, and now she's gone. I miss her so much that sometimes it is a physical ache. Sometimes, though, I can smell her perfume on the air. Jamie says it is just the scent of roses from the garden, but I refuse to listen to his ten-year-old logic. I prefer to imagine that she is here with me, standing just out of sight. Just out of reach.

At night, I close my eyes and I'm ten years old. I remember the softness of her cheek against my skin when she held me close, and the way she used to wrap me in a soft towel when I came out of the sea, chilled and salty. We spent a lot of time on the beach when I was younger. Most afternoons during the long school holidays, we would take the ten-minute walk through the town, over the swing bridge, and then onto the sand, mingling with the holiday makers. She would sit on an old grey blanket, knitting or reading or sometimes just watching the crowds. I would try to dig a hole to Australia or make a speedboat from sand that in my mind would whisk me away to exotic places. Funny how I spent all those years longing to get away, yet now I long to have just one more day sitting on

**116**

the sand, enjoying her company, and knowing that the treat of walking home with her was still ahead of me.

Outside my window, a gull cries out, and then they rise as one, taking wing on invisible thermals, diving and dancing in wild celebration – graceful, yet harsh. I'm captured by the beauty of their display. They wheel and spin, and fill the air with their mournful cries. And suddenly I know why they've come. It is no accident. No random act of nature. They've come to pay tribute to a woman who lived by the sea all her life, one of their own. She is gone, but never forgotten. The seagulls know that as well as I. But unlike me, they have not tried to hide away. Instead they've taken to the air, alive, vibrant, and so very beautiful.

And then, as suddenly as they arrived, they are gone. Who knows what current of wind drew them away. I stare out of the window, hoping for one last glimpse of dazzling white, but there's nothing to see except the brown tiles on the roof opposite, and the grey monochrome of a wintry sky.

There's a tentative knock at the door. "Mum?" Jamie sidles into the room, still in his pyjamas. His gaze flicks to my computer, and then guiltily he looks at me. "I know you said not to disturb you, but there's no bread for lunch."

I glance at my watch. I'm surprised to see it's nearly one o'clock. No bread? I know there's a loaf or two in the freezer, and I'm about to tell him so, but the wildness of the seagulls is infectious. Suddenly I don't want to eat a sandwich at my desk while my son continues his imaginary space adventure alone. I smile at him. "I tell you what, why don't we go into town and have lunch at the coffee shop?"

"Really?" His eyes widen, and he darts another look at my desk. "I thought you were going to be busy all day today."

"I was, and I do have a lot to do, but you know what? Today is a special day."

"It is?"

I nod. "Do you remember Grandma?"

"Of course." His expression turns wary.

A sharp pang of remorse cuts through me. In burying my grief, I've not allowed him to voice his own. Selfish? Oh yes, I have been very selfish, and in more ways then one. But not any more. "Today was Grandma's birthday. I think she'd like us to go and eat cake in memory of her. Would you be okay with that?"

He stares at me for a long moment and then smiles. "I think she'd like that a lot." Suddenly he seems taller, as though a weight has lifted from his shoulders.

"Go get dressed then."

"'kay." He turns happily towards the door, but then pauses. "Mum?"

"Yes?"

"Did you see the gulls just now?"

"Yes, I did." The memory of their acrobatics makes me smile.

Jamie grins in response. "Grandma once told me seagulls were her favourite bird. I think she would've liked seeing them too."

I nod, and breathe in the scent of summer roses that is suddenly filling the room. "Somehow, I think Grandma did."

*Author's note: I grew up in a small seaside town on the East coast of Engand. The harsh cries of seagulls and the mournful tones of fishing boat foghorns were part of my childhood landscape. Even now, these sounds will readily evoke memories of the past.*

*When my mother passed away, just as a new century began, I found the 22nd of November, her birthday, to be both a time of remembrance and sadness. How to celebrate the birth of someone no longer physically present? Then one grey November day, the seagulls arrived unexpectedly in the Midlands town where I now live. This story was the result – a tribute to a very special woman: my mother.*

## Rock Touch

*Author's note: I adore science fiction and science fantasy. This final story was an early attempt to break into this genre. Some time later I turned the story into a novel, which attracted some interest, but has yet to be published. One day I'll find the time to edit and polish it. Meanwhile, I hope you enjoy this venture into speculative fiction.*

The groan rolled across the landscape like a ripple on a lake.

Within seconds of its birth Tanar was aware of its presence moving towards her. She tried to react, tried to probe mentally for the source, but she was too slow. It overwhelmed her, deluging her senses with a blanket of sound, forcing her to throw up her defences. Then, as fast as it came, it was gone. Her field instruments discarded and forgotten, she scrambled to her feet and peered intently into the growing night, hoping irrationally that her eyes would catch the tail of the tremor. Was that it, over there? A shimmer spreading through the irregular terrain, dying as it rolled out to the far hills. She sighed and rubbed wearily at the brow over her right eye. A headache was forming.

As she turned, she saw her team of field geologists was gazing up at her, surprise and concern on their faces. Grant, her personal assistant, opened his mouth to speak but she silenced him with an imperative gesture of her hands. Straining her senses, Tanar probed the silence that had swallowed the disturbance, still willing herself to catch some last echo.

Suddenly she became aware that the team members were exchanging the kind of amused looks that suggested they thought she was nuts. She glared, pinpointing individuals with cold stares. The grins dropped quickly. "Didn't anyone feel anything?" she demanded.

Warned by the sharpness in her tone the crew answered with polite, formal negatives. Tanar sighed inwardly. This was the fourth time she had experienced the groaning cries on this new planet and each time the crew had denied hearing anything. Now her initial surprise was turning to unease; each cry was growing louder and more intense than the previous one. She had almost tasted a physical pain in the touch of that last keening ripple of sound, so intense was its grip on her. If only she knew what it was? And why it seemed to be singling her out.

She gazed out across the alien landscape once more, sure that the source of the disturbance was out there, somewhere. Worse, she was afraid that the crew were drawing near to it with each day that they extended their survey of the planet. She tried to shrug off the fear that chilled her skin. She'd seen plenty of strange things in her time as a planetary geologist. What difference did one more make? Get a grip, she told herself severely, and picking up her notepad she focused grimly back on the job at hand.

As soon as the day's samples had been catalogued and packed away, Tanar left the camp and headed out into the open. She felt uncharacteristically restless; the company of the crew had grated on her nerves throughout the day. Nevertheless, safety was foremost in her mind and she kept the camp's lights clearly in view as she walked. Before her the dominant sun of the alien star system was disappearing behind the horizon, leaving the irregular bulks of rocky outcrops silhouetted against the glowing sky. She reached the first of a series of steep hillocks and climbed slowly to its summit. Her heavy boots rasped against the gravel surface as she laboriously gained height. When at last the gravel gave way to solid rock she gave a sigh of relief, and stepped onto the crystalline surface.

A scream stabbed through her with an intensity of sound that drove her to her knees. With a cry of anguish she rammed her hands over her ears trying to block out the noise. The cry seemed to grow within her mind as she fought to escape it. Tears rolled unheeded down her face as she collapsed onto the rockface, curling into a tight fetal-like ball, seeking relief from the onslaught. Somehow above the turmoil she could hear her own voice calling out, begging for the pain to stop.

Words formed in her mind. 'Boots. Remove. Boots.' And with them came a compelling need to obey the command.

Desperately her fingers tore at the stubborn laces of the stiff black field boots she favoured. Disorientated by the howl of noise, it seemed forever before the boots were finally free and she hurled them from the rock.

With sudden abruptness, the noise released her. Drawing in gulps of cold, damp air she lay motionless, her hands still clamped over her ears and her face buried in the dirt. How long she remained like that she was uncertain. When she did finally move, it was with caution and an acute awareness of aching muscles and protesting sinews. Slowly she lifted her face from the earth and eased herself into a sitting position.

She frowned; something else was wrong. She stared down at the palms of her hands trying to identify the problem. The excess of noise was still affecting her thoughts, making it difficult to focus her mind. She touched her cheeks slowly, brushing away the loose earth that had clung to her. Her skin tingled with a subtle warmth that did not belong to the chill of the evening. *Odd, so very odd.* She looked again at her hands, and an idea began to form at the edge of her consciousness. From her hands her attention shifted warily to the crystalline surface she was resting on. An idea formed that contradicted her scientific knowledge, yet was strangely compelling. Cautiously she reached out and pressed her palms against the rock face. A tremor of heat glowed through her fingertips, racing up the nerves in a flow of warmth.

Shocked she snatched her hands away and felt the contact break with an abrupt snap.

The air shifted around her as if a crowd of people had moved past her. The atmosphere grew tense and heavy. Almost at once Tanar was aware of a feeling of regret. It was as if she had harmed somebody with calculated ease and now it was too late to repay the hurt. The oppressive emotion weighed down on her, bringing fresh tears to her eyes. She shook her head, trying to throw off the emotion. Part of her was still aware of her position, sitting alone on the rock. She was being manipulated and controlled by something outside of herself, and with a shock of fear, she realised she was powerless to prevent who or what it was that had invaded her body.

Curiously she watched as her hand lifted itself from her lap, then with a growing sense of horror she sat transfixed as it reached down to the surface of the rock. As her fingers brushed against the crystalline surface she desperately tried to break free of the physical lassitude that had descended on her. In desperation she tried to pull away, but her muscles were locked. Her palm dropped flat against the surface and the contact gripped her. Unable to resist Tanar sank into the consciousness of the alien rock.

She woke, teeth chattering with cold, and nausea roiling in her stomach. She tried to turn, hoping to ease the cramp which gnawed at her. Solid rock grazed against her skin. She peered up, seeing grey stone inches from her face and feeling it hard against her back.

She realised she was in a narrow rock crevice, cocooned on all sides. Cool air moved across her face, though, and she lifted her head to savour the freshness of it in her lungs. The alien landscape stretched before her, reminding her of the African plains that she had once called home. Her eyes strained in the dim light of early morning as, for one crazy moment, she imagined there were gazelle grazing just out of sight. Where on earth was she? And how had she managed to wedge herself into such a tight space? Slowly she worked her hand free, her cramped muscles protesting at every movement. Then, with more effort than she had expected to use, she managed to push herself out of the rock's grasp. She sprawled inelegantly on the ground, sweat cooling on her skin, her breath laboured.

She lay still, allowing the pins and needles to run their course. Memory of how she came to be here still eluded her as she pulled herself to her feet. There was something familiar about the rock face beneath her feet but she could not remember what. She felt chilled to the bone and incredibly weary. And where the hell were her boots?

She stretched her aching back, studying the alien landscape around her, and then caught sight of her footwear. The boots were lying half-way down a steep scree slope, as though casually discarded and unwanted.

Memory flashed.

Camp! She whirled round in sudden panic as the thought hit her. To her relief the lights of the generator were flickering brightly. More memories surfaced. She'd gone for a walk, she thought. *I came out for a walk and then* ... She looked at the narrow crevice. *I must have fallen asleep and* ... She shook her head in confusion; no way, would she have wriggled her way into such a small space. It almost looked at though the space had been moulded around a human body. Glancing up she saw the sun was rising quickly above the horizon. She glanced once more at the crevice, and then made her way down the scree slope, wincing at the jagged stones beneath her feet. Retrieving her boots, she quickly pulled them on, and then started to jog towards the camp, grateful for the warmth the exercise gave her.

"Where have you been?" demanded Grant angrily as she arrived on the camp's perimeter. "You were missing all

123

night. I didn't know whether to send out a search party or whether you'd done it on purpose."

"You should have assumed that I was lost," Tanar snapped. "Don't they teach you anything in field school these days?"

"They teach us not to leave camp alone," Grant retorted.

She opened her mouth to speak, but then changed her mind. In his present mood Grant would not understand the unexplained events of the night.

"You're lucky to be alive," Grant continued, staring at her suspiciously. "It was below zero last night, you know."

"All the more reason for you to have come looking for me," she snapped. He made a dismissive sound, and walked away. She watched him go, his words adding to her confusion. Below zero? How could that be? Now she was back in the camp she felt no effects from her night in the open, yet if Grant was telling the truth she should be experiencing third degree exposure. She pushed the problem from her mind. She was fine, and had more important concerns, like getting the crew out into the field.

"Okay? Everybody ready?" Tanar swung quickly into her morning routine. "Today we are heading along the western trajectory and then doubling back on ourselves five kilometres northwards. So, by nightfall we should be over there."

She pointed to their intended destination, realising as she did so that they would end the day approximately by the rock where she had woken.

"Tanar?" one of the crew called impatiently. "Are you going to stand there gawping at the landscape all day?"

She shook her head, realising she had drifted into thought. "Sorry. Right, today's assignments will be as follows."

The day dragged slowly as the crew worked through the routines of geological surveying. Even with recent advances in technical analysis much of the initial field classification was still done by eye. A mobile analytical unit gave the team an instant chemical breakdown of the bulk of the rock, but the mineral composition was left to human judgement. Each outcrop was carefully mapped by hand before the coordinates were locked into the field computer's memory. As Tanar had forecast it was nearly dusk when they reached the final outcrop.

"Last one for today," said Grant, with relief, standing at the base of an exposed surface. "I'll get a fresh specimen."

He pulled his handlaser from his belt and turned towards a protruding cluster of dark tangerine crystals, clearing intending to slice off a clean surface.

"Wait a minute!" Tanar ran to catch up with him, driven by an unexplainable impulse to prevent him from cutting into the rock. She stooped down and picked up a jagged boulder the size of her hand that was lying loose. "This will do."

Grant stared at her in disbelief. "Are you serious?" he asked. "You know that loose rock isn't representative. Come on, Tanar, even a zero-level candidate knows that."

"Yes, of course." Tanar dropped the boulder, embarrassed. She held out her hand for the laser. "Just kidding. Look I'll finish off here. You go and start camp."

Grant studied her for a long moment, his expression concerned. "I don't think you're well, Tanar. You've been acting weird ever since we got here. Why don't you go and rest."

"Grant …"

He shook his head, refusing to listen. "The team has been talking, Tanar. There's talk of contacting control about you. Now, if you don't want that to happen, I suggest you take *my* advice – go and rest." Without waiting for her to reply he turned to the rockface and slashed the brilliant white laser beam through its surface.

Tanar heard the scream erupt from her lungs as the pain resonated through her. She launched herself towards the cause of her agony, dragging Grant to the ground. For an instant she grappled for the handlaser, but then another wave of pain struck her and she cried out again. In desperation she rolled across the dirt, clinging to Grant, and trying to burn out the threatening darkness.

Above crashing waves of sound she could hear her name being called, repeated continuously in frantic pitches. Hands pulled her back, forcing her to fight against their restraint with a wild fury. She felt an arm lock around her throat, cutting off the air from her body; then there was the taste of blood in her mouth as she bit into flesh. Abruptly she was thrown against raw rock. Cold crystal jarred against her skin, breaking into her nightmare. The touch held her, washing away the anger and the pain. As she ceased to struggle against the hold, the darkness flooded over her, removing the image of her destruction.

Pulsating rhythm echoed through her mind, forming coloured shapes of sound which drifted away into the envelope of black silence around her. She clawed her way through an intangible world seeking for a reality to cling to. Terror rose and died and the rhythm went on.

'Dadh, tadh, tadh, tanah, tanar … Tanar!'

She sensed her name rather than heard it and became aware of its steady beat being caught up by other tones and voices around her. She tried to turn towards the name but was trapped in a directionless void.

"I hear you," she cried. "I hear you."

Sensations swooped down on her with hungry claws as the alien consciousness leapt at her response. She fell into the touch of the rock, unable to resist the strength of its contact. Deeper and deeper she was drawn into the inner world, touching the ways of a life form that did not share her senses. In one incredible instant she was transformed into a world of silicon intelligence. She breathed the same white fire of living diamonds and tasted the flame of a

126

thousand sapphires. Vast crystalline structures danced in honour to her, displaying a rainbow of emotions like a kaleidoscope.

At last she was released from the inward pull and with relief she drew away from the touch. She felt awed by the scenes that had played before her. Beauty from another world still filled her thoughts. For an instant she wanted to run, to forget the wonders that could never exist in her life, but the creature was waiting for her to reciprocate experience. She had been within the inner veil of an alien culture and now she was required to return the experience. As she comprehended the intentions of the rock she felt panic seize her. The grip grew tighter around her and Tanar realised that she had nowhere to run to.

Half-forgotten memories floated through her mind. She remembered her mother; a tall, boisterous woman with a flare for physics. Her father's face focused sharply before her; his fine features so like her own. She cried as a baby in her parents arms, learned to walk and talk; growing in strength and intelligence. Piece by piece she relieved her life, recalling bad and good with a frightening clarity. She was at once watching and living the memories.

Tanar rested, sipping the cool silence, aware of the mind that waited beyond the shadows. The sharing was over and she could sense the alien's unsureness. She longed to reach out to him. She realised that she assigned a human gender to him without thinking. I have lived with you, she thought. Speak to me. I need you.

She felt calmness brush against her nerves, removing the last traces of tension that clung to her. Images floated through her mind as the creature sought a new form of communication. Eagerly she reached towards them. With a sharp abruptness, as if a sheet of ice had suddenly shattered, the images broke away, and in their place voices began to sound in her head. First one, then another, and another, each clamouring for her attention: "Tanar. Oh,

127

Tanar. What have we done?" "We are one. Can you not feel the bond?" "It must be broken. How foolish. Forgive me, Tanar. Forgive us."

"I don't understand," Tanar said, her voice betraying her anxiety. "What is there to forgive?"

"We sought you out," it said. "We wanted to learn about this creature that we found wandering on the surface of our world. We didn't realise what the linking of our lives would mean. Tanar, please …"

"Stop it!" Tanar cried as a wave of communal grief crashed over her. "We are one now. What we just shared, it was amazing. There is no sorrow here."

"No," the voices continued sadly. "We have seen. Your people seek after our kind for wealth. Minerals to you are power and money. To us they are body and life, they are kin."

"No," she said, desperately. "We use rocks not…" Words failed her. How could she explain? "On my world, crystalline structures such as you, they have no feelings. They aren't sentient. They don't live like you."

"Your people cannot see, Tanar. Only you could we touch. Our people must withdraw from yours. Forgive us. We have shared with you, but it is a sharing in which we cannot live, we cannot be. Forgive us."

Tanar was suddenly alone. The voices in her head silenced. Dazed, she stared at the face of the rock before her, trying to comprehend all that had just happened. Turning slowly, she saw Grant slumped unconscious on the ground. She dropped to his side, checking for a pulse. He groaned softly and began to regain consciousness. She glanced back at the rest of the team. They too were unconscious, but slowly stirring. From her casual glance, they seemed unharmed, and instinctively she knew that they had suffered no significant hurt.

For the first time since she'd arrived on the planet, she felt completely and utterly free of the alien presence. Tears welled in her eyes at the depth of her loss. It was as if somebody had removed all her most treasured memories. The emptiness grew hollower as she brushed her fingers against the rock and felt nothing – no warmth, no sentience, just smooth crystal. Not wanting to believe the truth she threw herself against its surface. It felt cold and lifeless to her touch.

"Listen to me," she sobbed. "I can tell them. I'll make them realise. There must be others who can touch you. Please, don't leave me."

Around her the field crew began to stir.

"Speak to me," she implored the alien. "They'll think I'm … mad."

Was that what the creature had seen? Her story would appear insane to those who could not feel the touch. Those who paid for planetary exploration would merely see rocks of high mineral value and a geologist who had been driven mad by too many long weeks in space.

She was aware as she turned to face the crew of the faintest tremor beneath her feet. Grabbing one of the discarded field instruments, she sucked in a sharp breath as she saw the readings on the meter. Horrified she recognised the danger that faced the team even as she understood the protective imperative driving the tremors.

With one final caress, she pushed herself from the rock and ran to Grant's side. He gazed up at her, his eyes focusing slowly. "What the hell happened?" he asked. He struggled to sit up, succeeding with her help.

"We have to get away from here," she said urgently. She held up the instrument so he could see for himself. "There's going to be one hell of an earthquake."

## Acknowledgements

*Musical Memories*, *The Walker* and *Chalk and Cheese* were first published in People's Friend.

*The Good Example*, *When is it my turn?* and *Afraid* were first published in Christian Woman.

*The Homecoming* was first published in Red Letter.

*The Waiting Game* was first published in Just Seventeen.

*Rock Touch* was first published in Imagine.

Printed in the United Kingdom
by Lightning Source UK Ltd.
134581UK00001B/172-198/P

9 780956 097408